EYELINER & ALIBIS

BEAUTY SECRETS MYSTERY 3

STEPHANIE DAMORE

PINK SAPPHIRE PRESS

To my mom,
For always answering your phone.
Thank you.

1

I sat and analyzed my reflection in the mirror. *Sweet sugar. What color lipstick is this?* I knew it wasn't a Beauty Secrets shade. I had their entire catalog memorized even if I wasn't selling much of it anymore. I smiled and looked up at the makeup artist. If this was the price I had to pay to be on TV, then it was worth it.

As it turned out, the wife of the CEO of the Daily Shopping Channel loved my skincare line, Sugar & Sass. I was thrilled to get a call from the station manager, asking *me* to fill in for a last-minute cancellation. The business-minded voice in my head had convinced me to jump at the opportunity, but the rest of me was having second thoughts. My knees bounced and my whole body quivered. I would've killed for some chocolate right about then.

"You'll do great."

I turned to the sweet redhead sitting in the makeup chair next to me. Unlike me, she looked relaxed and simply allowed the artist to do her job. I had questioned every shade choice and application technique. I recognized the woman from the morning program, but I couldn't recall her name. Heck, at that moment, my own name escaped me. Thankfully, I wasn't alone on this trip. Finn had driven me to Tampa for this interview, and was waiting outside the door for me to finish getting ready.

"Being on TV is always nerve-wracking the first time or two, but I'm sure you'll do great. I have to tell you, most of us are also fans."

The makeup artist nodded and then opened her bag to reveal my facial line of lotions and scrubs.

I smiled like a kid preparing to eat birthday cake. It was true, my fan base was growing by the day. Business was booming and I couldn't stock inventory fast enough, to the point that I even considered outsourcing production, something I thought wouldn't have been financially possible for a long time.

The door opened and my heart dropped into my stomach as I thought I was being called on set, but that wasn't the case. In sauntered Tess Hill, the Queen of the Daily Shopping Channel. Only she didn't look like the polished royal she appeared to be on TV. Her white linen suit fit the part just fine, but her accessories were questionable—oversized sunglasses sitting crookedly on her face and a martini sloshing in her hand. The woman tumbled into my lap while trying to take a seat in front of her own vanity. Miraculously, she managed to keep her drink upright.

"Where did you come from?" she said to me, as if it were my fault I was sitting there.

"Sorry." I offered her a shove up. She steadied herself with a hand on my shoulder and plopped down next to me, raising her finger for a makeup artist to touch up her look.

"Hi, Tess, how are you doing today?" the redhead asked.

"Oh, shut up, Claire." Tess whipped off her sunglasses and threw them on the counter.

"*That's it – Claire!*" I almost blurted out. Both Claire and her makeup artist raised their eyebrows in the mirror to one another. I sincerely hoped Tess wouldn't be the one interviewing me. In fact, I hoped she wouldn't be going on the air anytime soon. The woman was a train wreck.

The next knock on the door was for me. Skip was ready for me to come on set. I quickly learned that everyone referred to him as *Skip the Producer*, as if a lot of men named Skip worked around there, or as if he were John the Baptist or something. Skip was a sight in his white lab coat with a headset sticking out of his mess of dark curls. I secretly wondered if his curls were naturally that tight or if he'd had a professional perm.

I checked my appearance in the mirror once more and sucked in a deep breath before standing to follow him. Claire reached over and squeezed my hand.

"Remember, you'll do great. I only wish I were the one lucky enough to interview you."

"Thanks, that's sweet of you." I wished that as well. I reached up to touch the gold cross around my neck, a habit I used to calm my nerves, only to realize it wasn't there. I frantically searched on the floor, checked my pockets, traced the collar of my shirt, but it was nowhere to be seen. The necklace had belonged to my nana and had only recently been gifted to me through her sister, my great aunt Margot. She said she had a feeling her sister had wanted me to have it, so now it was mine. That didn't surprise me. I thought of my nana as my guardian angel and talked to her all the time. I could totally see her pushing her sister's subconscious to gift me the piece.

Skip the Producer looked impatient, pulling a pocket

watch out of his lab coat to check the time. I felt a panic attack coming on, but what could I do? It was show time.

Finn stood to the side, off set. I gave him a shaky smile. He grinned back, exuding the confidence that I coveted in that moment. I gave myself a quick internal pep talk. I had this. This was my moment to show the world Sugar & Sass. I knew my products were awesome, and soon millions of other people would know it too.

I closed my eyes and took a couple of calming breaths, but I had way too much energy to sit still. I would've preferred to start bouncing around like a boxer ready to step into the ring, and I would've if I hadn't worried people would think I was a psycho. Instead, I took another steadying breath and turned my attention toward the segment preceding mine. My eyes brightened at the man dressed head to toe in Kelly green. Wow! Now there was a way to get noticed. The host running his segment seemed to think so too. She must've found a way to touch him a handful of times in the short time I watched—whether it was brushing his arm, or touching him playfully on the shoulder while laughing at some offhanded comment he made. My brow furrowed as I tried to figure out what he was even selling—surely not his wardrobe, or his personality.

It turned out to be neither one of those things. It was a "revolutionary" multi-use gardening tool—a shovel, planter, and spade all in one! I curiously waited for the demonstration. The host looked like she hadn't gardened a day in her life, not with those long, polished fingernails and Louboutin heels of hers. The only place she probably ever got dirty was between the sheets. Even the guy seemed to blush at the overt attention. I turned away from the spectacle and mentally regrouped for my segment.

I had been invited to promote my facial line, which

included a face wash, scrub, and moisturizer. I was going over the ingredients and benefits of my organic line in my head when Skip the Producer nodded to me that it was time to go. I looked over at Finn. He was shoving a chocolate-chip cookie in his mouth with one hand and holding a Coke in the other. The man could probably eat the whole platter of cookies and still have a six-pack. *So* not fair! He took a swig of his Coke and raised his eyebrows at me over the can. That look could mean several different things—anything from, "*Hey, sexy,*" to "*You want one?*" I nodded back to him as if to say, "*Later.*" T-minus twenty minutes and then my beau and I would begin our vacation, soaking up the southern Florida sun. Picturing Finn shirtless got me flustered for an entirely different reason. I just had to get this madness over with. My stomach rolled and I prayed I wouldn't vomit on national television. I reached for my cross again and came up empty, so I clasped my hands in front of me to keep them from shaking as I followed Skip the Producer on set.

"And who's this *chica*?" The sideways glance the host tossed my way told me it wasn't meant as a term of endearment. She took a nail file out of her back pocket and began working on her nails.

I smiled politely anyway while Skip the Producer introduced us.

"This is Ziva Diaz. She's the brains behind Sugar & Sass."

The woman never looked up from her nails.

"And this is Marissa Morrison," Skip filled in for her. "You two will be doing the segment together. Do you have any questions?" I shook my head even though I had about a million. Starting with, *Why me? Why her?*

"Marissa, you?"

"Just two. What does she make, and why do I care?" The

host stopped filing just long enough to eye me up. I wanted to punch her in the face.

Skip the Producer rolled his eyes. "Why don't you just give us a minute," he said to me. "Just stand right there. See the X?" I moved to center stage where he had motioned. "Yes, perfect. We'll be right with you." *Maybe I should just bolt now?* I looked for the neon exit sign. A stagehand worked to switch out the set, replacing the garden tool and potting soil with clear acrylic cubes of various heights, with my products placed on top. A jar of honey and a sprig of lavender accented the table.

Marissa joined me on set a moment later. A makeup artist attempted to touch up her lipstick, but one evil eye had the woman retreating in a hot second. I glanced at the exit once more.

And then a miracle happened. The cameras started rolling, and Marissa did a one-eighty. I had never seen a person flick a switch on their personality so quickly. It was downright scary. I stood there dumbfounded as Little Miss Sunshine greeted me on set with a warm handshake and a winning smile for the cameras. Jekyll and Hyde, she was.

"Well, ladies, are you in for a treat today. I have Ziva Diaz with me. She's the founder of the ah-mazing skincare line called Sugar & Sass. Now, if you haven't had the chance to try out her products, then you don't know what you're missing! I, for one, love them." Marissa looked to me to continue.

I cleared my throat. "Thank you, Marissa. When I started this business, I had a single goal in mind."

"To make money?" Marissa laughed into the camera.

"Um, no. To create a skincare line that people could feel good about using. In fact, all of our products contain certified organic ingredients, so you can feel good about using anything we offer."

"So true. Ladies, you would be amazed to see all the chemicals that are in your traditional beauty regimen." From the way Marissa's face reflected unnaturally off the studio lighting, I had a feeling she didn't care what was in her beauty regimen as long as it made her look good, but she told a good story.

"Ladies, what we have for you today is Sugar & Sass's best-selling skincare kit, which includes the facial cleanser, scrub, and moisturizer for the incredible price of fifty-five dollars. Now, quantities are limited, so get your order in right away. The phone lines are open. And if you have any questions, feel free to call in. Oh, we have a caller right now. Hi, Margaret from Savannah."

"Oh my goodness. Am I on? I am? Hi, Marissa. Hi, Ziva. I'm so excited!" The woman squealed into the phone. I plastered on my megawatt and mega-fake smile. Marissa, however, took it all in stride. "We're excited too! Have you used the products before?" she asked, encouraging conversation.

"I have, and I just have to say, Ziva, I love them. You do an amazing job. I already have this set, but I'm ordering another one, just to make sure I never run out!"

"Awesome. Thank you so much," I replied. The lady clicked off and Marissa kept going. "Margaret is just one of the dozens of people who have already called in. Thank you all. You can see on the screen that we've already sold about half of the stock available."

We did? Awesome. I looked around to see where Marissa was getting the information from when I spotted her ear piece. That had to be it.

"And don't forget, you can also order online. The website and product number is right here on the side of your screen." I did the looking-around thing again. I really needed to stop doing that on TV.

"Ziva, why don't you tell our viewers a little more about how you created your formulas?"

"Well, I developed everything in my own home."

Marissa picked up a jar of moisturizer and read the back of the label for the first time. Her countenance immediately changed. "Almond oil, beeswax, shea butter? And people actually pay you for this?"

Wait, wha—? Hadn't she just said that she loved it?

The hostess picked up the scrub next and read the back of that one as well. "Sugar? You seriously put sugar in this? What, from your pantry?"

"It's not white sugar, it's—" *Wait, what the heck am I doing?* When did this become a defense trial?

"Looks like you can buy these ingredients at the grocery store and make this stuff at home. All I really see here is a pretty package." Marissa stared me down, begging me to call her bluff.

I looked left and right, trying to find someone to help me out here, but I was on my own. "Um, yes and no, I guess." I scrambled for words to defend my product on national television. "All of my products are free-trade, organic, and locally sourced wherever possible. The packaging is just a bonus." I winked at the camera and tried not to glare at Marissa.

"But you *can* make this at home," she reiterated. Skip the Producer popped up on stage right, making the cut motion with his hand across his neck. Marissa ignored him and stared at me, waiting for me to keep going.

"Sure, but I'd say you could make just about anything at home, am I right? People make chocolate-chip cookies at home all the time, but that doesn't stop bakeries from making them."

"And it looks like you *love* your cookies," Marissa said with a smirk.

Oh no she didn't. "Excuse me?"

"Are we done here?" Marissa asked to no one in particular. Skip the Producer nodded his head, with his face was buried in his hand. "Great." Marissa flung her note card in the air and started to walk off stage.

A huffy-looking man in an expensive suit greeted her. "What the hell was that all about?" he demanded in a gruff British accent.

"Suck it, Rupert," she spat over her shoulder and kept on walking. The man's complexion turned from ruddy to crimson and I thought he might have a stroke. I wouldn't have let her get away that easily. In fact, *I* wasn't done with her either.

"Ziva, wait." Skip tried to stop me, but I sidestepped him. "I'm really sorry about this," he shouted to my back.

I rounded on him. "You're sorry? Seriously. That's all you got? That woman is unhinged, and you knew that. She made me look ridiculous! Not to mention, she was rude and insulting!" I looked around the stage for Marissa, but she had already made her exit. I stormed off the side of the stage and almost ran right into Finn.

"Babe."

"Don't babe me," I snapped at my beau. I was seeing red. Finn's color drained and I checked myself. "Sorry. You know I'm not mad at you."

"Yeah, I know. What do you say I buy you a drink?"

I thought about it for second. "And some truffles?"

"And some truffles."

~

I POPPED two of the chocolates into my mouth and sighed at the chocolatey goodness. It was my equivalent of slugging back a shot of whiskey. I rummaged around the patisserie box for one more. It had been over an hour since the stunt and I was still furious, but the truffles helped me hold my tongue.

"How bad was it?" I asked Finn as he parked the truck at The Tiki Hut. I smiled at his choice of establishment. Putting my toes in the sand with a drink in hand was just what I needed.

"Ah, it wasn't that bad. Truth? She made herself look like an ass more than anything."

"Really?"

"Yeah, babe. No doubt she'll be canned."

That made me feel better.

"What was up with her anyway?"

"I have no idea. She was witchy before the segment and then sweet as can be once the cameras started rolling, until she flipped again." I shrugged my shoulders and eyed the patisserie box once more.

"Don't worry about it. You heard that woman who called in. Your patrons love you and your products. If anything, you'll sell more because of her stunt." I hoped he was right. "Trust me," Finn said, giving me his winning grin as he reached for my hand.

"You know, I'd better call and check in with the store, make sure everything's all right." Izzy, my astrology-loving manager, had a Zen-like attitude that served her and my store well. Like I said, business was booming and I was making bank, thanks in part to her intuition. I knew she could hold down the fort, but I still liked to check in from time to time. I let go of Finn's hand and went for my phone in my purse, but came up empty. I looked around Finn's truck and checked my pockets, even though there was no way it could've fit in my Bermuda shorts.

"What is happening to me today?" I practically growled. "First my cross, and now my phone? I'm losing everything!"

"You lost your cross?"

"I don't want to talk about it," I shot back.

"O-kay," Finn looked like he was about to take the closest exit and wish me good luck with everything … like, life.

"We're going to have to go back," I said softer this time. I needed to quit snapping at the man.

"Any chance you left it at the hotel?"

"None. I checked my email while waiting for my makeup. In fact, that's probably where it is." The last place I wanted to go was back to the studio, but what choice did I have? I needed my phone. In the meantime, I borrowed Finn's to make the call.

"Sugar and Sass, this is Izzy," my manager's voice chimed on the other line.

"Hey, Izzy, it's Ziva."

"I don't know what happened to you, love, but I have been trying to get a hold of you. I just had the worst feeling ever." What did I tell you? She's good.

"I don't even know where to begin, but it was a total disaster. I'll fill you in later. Just please tell me that everything is awesome with the store."

"Yeah, no worries here."

I could hear Izzy clicking away on her cell phone. "You're Googling me, aren't you?" I asked.

"Hey, I thought I was the psychic?"

I rolled my eyes at Izzy's reply, praying that Marissa's

stunt hadn't already hit the air waves. "Okay, well, I'll leave you to that. I don't think I want to know what you find. I'll check back in later. Cool?"

"Oh my goodness." I had a feeling Izzy had just struck Internet gold. "Ziva—a"

"I know, like I said, a disaster."

"You poor girl. I'll talk to you soon."

2

The parking lot was packed when we pulled back in. In fact, I was sure more cars were here now than before. Had a red carpet been rolled out? I vaguely remembered the women getting their hair and makeup done for some gala event tonight, but I hadn't cared to hear the details. Guess maybe I should've paid attention?

I recognized *Entertainment Now* reporter Cee Cee Thomas standing in front of a camera, lights shining behind her. A backdrop with a repeated pattern of the company's logo and an oversized heart in the middle took up part of the walk way. Photographers were at the ready, snapping pics as guests made their entrances.

Tess Hill stepped out of a black limo, looking much more put together than she had earlier this afternoon. It's amazing how a few hours could sober up a person. She posed in front of the backdrop like a pro—hand on her hip, head cocked slightly. She wore her blond hair long, her red dress tight, and her cleavage high. *Subtle* wasn't in her vocabulary. I looked down at my wardrobe. Maybe I could pass as the wait staff?

Tess walked the carpet solo, but just behind her was Sterling Gomez walking hand-in-hand with a beautiful blonde. I assumed she was his wife. If Tess Hill was the queen of DSC, then he was the king. The two had been co-hosts of the network's most prominent programming for years, decades really. My nana had been a huge fan. Heck, I'd even consider myself a fan. He had a certain charisma that made him attractive to women of all ages. Why couldn't he have been the one to interview me? I almost sighed at what could've been.

"What do you want to do?" Finn asked, snapping me out of it.

"I think I should be able to sneak back in. The building's obviously open. It shouldn't take me long."

"Okay, I'll just circle around and keep an eye out for you."

"Sounds good. I'll just be a minute," I said as I shut the truck door. Famous last words.

The bubbly receptionist who had greeted me this afternoon was long gone. Standing in her place was the same company logo and heart backdrop. The impressive piece blocked her desk and sectioned off the rest of the space. The red carpet extended in front of it and up the stairs, where the upper lobby's lights sparkled and the champagne flowed. People mingled in the space, with their glittery dresses and black ties. I spotted Claire, or more specifically, her dress. The mint-green cocktail dress, with its sweetheart neckline and bubble skirt, was beautiful. Paired with her fiery hair color and fair skin, her wardrobe choice was perfect. I had a sudden, overwhelming urge to go shopping. *Maybe tomorrow.*

Lights flashed and all the glitz and glam distracted me for a few moments until I remembered why I was there. I snuck behind the backdrop and headed toward the side offices. Not a soul was in sight. I weaved my way down the darkened hallway, trying to make it back to the green room where I had spent most of my time earlier. This time, the doors were locked.

"Well, crud." I surveyed my options. If I recalled, the first floor of the building was basically a rectangle with the reception up front, offices down one side, and the studio down the other with the dressing rooms along the back. I could backtrack through the front lobby, cut through the studio, and make my way to the back rooms, and hopefully my phone. I crossed my fingers that the set would be accessible. As I walked back through the lobby, I almost smacked into Skip the Producer. It appeared we were both in a hurry. Skip had exchanged his lab coat for a lavender suit jacket. It was the most bizarre color choice for a black-tie event, but he made it work. He took a few steps backwards when he recognized me.

I held up my hands to show my innocence. "It's fine. I'm sorry about earlier."

He relaxed ever so slightly. "I'm sorry, too. I promise, that will never happen again."

"I appreciate that, but I don't plan on coming back."

"Understandable. I'll let you get to it then." I said goodbye and we both hurried off in opposite directions.

As I started sneaking toward the studio, I thought of the things we do for technology. Did I really need my phone that badly? I sighed. Yes. Yes, I did. I gave a shove to the studio's entrance and the double doors swung inward. The sets were dark with not a single stagehand or makeup artist in sight.

Cut through, get your phone, and get out, I told myself. My plan had been brilliant. I could almost picture my cell phone sitting on the vanity counter in the green room. That is, until I tripped over a pair of Louboutin high heels and landed on my face. I rolled onto my backside and turned to look at the body wearing those beautiful shoes. I recognized Marissa in an instant. If the pool of blood surrounding her, and the gardening tool sticking out of her back were any indication, she was definitely dead.

I'd like to think that I had grown some in the last year. The fact that I didn't feel like passing out or throwing up at finding a dead body testified to this. I calmly checked Marissa for a pulse—unsurprised by the result given her glassy eyes and horror-frozen face staring back at me—found a nearby landline, and called the police. I wondered if I should've notified someone official-looking. But who? The celebrities were pouring in, and I knew chaos would ensue as soon as they got word. I didn't think the police would want me tipping off the guests and causing a scene, so I called Finn instead. I probably should've given him a heads-up as he nearly choked on his words after he asked me what was up and saw Marissa's body lying there.

"Jesus, Ziva, what the hell happened? I thought you wanted to introduce me to someone famous, not hide a body."

"I didn't do this!" I snapped.

"Oh, um..."

"Nice. You see a dead body and think it's my fault. You should know better by now," I said with a laugh. Finn glanced my way as if to check my mental status. "I'm fine. Trust me. I'm okay. I just didn't want you to freak out when you saw the cavalry pull in. Do you think we should wait with her or meet the police up front?"

Finn looked at Marissa's body and shuddered. "Let's

meet them by the front door. You can tell the police where her body is and let them deal with crowd control."

Finn followed me as we weaved our way back to the entrance. A police officer met us in the back hallway, his gun drawn.

"Hands up!" he shouted. Finn immediately complied.

"WHAT?! No, you've got this all wrong," I started to say.

"I said 'hands up'!" the officer repeated as he stepped closer.

"Ziva!" Finn added.

"What? This is ridiculous!" I may have even stomped my foot. "WE called YOU. Put the gun down so you can help us."

"Ma'am, put your hands up."

"Idiot," I said to Finn with a shake of my head. In hindsight, it probably wasn't smart to pull attitude, but I was dumbfounded by the turn of events. I copied Finn and put my hands in the air.

"Get on the ground, NOW!" Sweat beaded on the officer's brow. I held my tongue as he commanded us to lie on our stomachs with our hands behind our backs.

"I told you, we called you. You need to let us go," I said to the officer over my shoulder as he handcuffed me. He clicked the cuffs even tighter. Finn had exercised his right to remain silent, and the look he gave me at that moment suggested I do the same.

It wasn't until I had been separated from Finn and unceremoniously dumped in the back of a police car, with cuffs digging into my skin and flashing lights circling around me, that I realized the seriousness of the situation. A similar circus played out around the car Finn occupied. Where was Detective Roxy, my Port Haven detective friend, when I needed her?

I wasn't left waiting for long. An older lady with spiky salt-and-pepper hair and hard-set eyes barked at the media to back off as she yanked open the squad car door and peered in at me.

"This is all just a misunderstanding," I said to the woman, who I assumed was a detective.

"Should I consider this your confession?" she said in a matter-of-fact voice.

"What? No! Why would you think that? I just found Marissa's body." Gosh, what was it with people thinking I'm a murderer?

"I see. Was she a friend of yours?"

"Not hardly," I said before filtering. "I mean, no, I just met her today."

"I see," the detective repeated.

"No, seriously. I was just on set trying to find my cell phone when I literally tripped right over her."

"You want to back it up for me?"

I thought for a second about how far back I wanted to go and how much detail I wanted to provide.

"I was a guest on the show today. While I was here, I left my cell phone in the green room. When I came back tonight to find it, I found Marissa instead." I wiggled my fingers and attempted to rotate my wrists. The fact that my hands were still bound behind my back intensified the pain. The detective took note of my discomfort, but didn't offer to loosen the cuffs. Instead, she continued her line of questioning.

"And what time would that have been?"

"I don't know, fifteen, twenty minutes ago? I called you guys as soon as I found her."

"Why didn't you alert anyone? Get help?"

"She was dead. I called you."

"How did you know she was dead?"

"It was pretty obvious, what with all the blood and that gardening-tool thingy sticking out of her back. Plus, I checked for a pulse."

"What did you say?"

"Um, I checked for a pulse? I know how you guys don't like people messing with your vics and all, but I wanted to make sure there wasn't anything I could do for her."

"You know all about that, huh?"

"Er..." I snapped my mouth shut and I could see the thoughts behind the detective's eyes. I was back to being *prime suspect number one*. I wondered if now was an appropriate time to drop Detective Roxy's name? Or maybe Detective Brandle's? My other detective buddy had since retired, but I was sure someone could get a hold of him. On second thought, did I want this woman to know this wasn't my first ride on the murder train? Would she find out eventually? Right now, all she knew was that I was a recent guest on the show, with a missing cell phone. Sure, my segment had been a disaster, but my background check was clear, well mostly clear, and I didn't think she'd have further reason to question me. Bottom line? I did not need to make her anymore suspicious.

"What's this gardening tool business?" the detective asked.

"Well, they say it's "revolutionary" but I'm pretty sure there are others on the market just like it." The detective looked at me like I had two heads. "Anyway, I saw it sticking out of her back and knew she wouldn't be walking away from that."

"Could you ID it again?"

I cocked my head, trying to figure out where this was going, but the detective didn't offer up any other info, so I answered her question, "Yeah, of course. The guy who makes them was on right before me. I saw his demo."

"Good. Now tell me, how did you enter the studio?"

"Through the side door?"

"It was unlocked?" The detective looked incredulous.

"Yes ma'am."

"You didn't find that odd?"

"Why would I? For all I knew, the studio was open twenty-four hours." Okay, so I knew the studio wasn't open twenty-four hours, but I was more concerned with retrieving my phone at the time. I didn't think the detective would buy that.

"Where's this cell phone of yours?" the detective asked, as if reading my thoughts.

I shrugged my shoulders. "Don't know. Never made it that far." Hashtag, true story.

"Sit tight," the woman said, motioning for me to scoot back so she could shut the car door.

"Can you please loosen these?" My fingers were starting to tingle.

"In a minute," she said and then shut the door. I saw her walk away and have a mini pow-wow with a couple of other uniformed officers. Finn was standing just to the side, chatting up a group of EMTs as if they were best buddies. I was instantly irked at the injustice of it all. I watched the police set up a barricade, making the media stand behind it, and I wondered how in the world they'd go about interviewing all the guests inside and onsite. *What a mess.* I found that if I focused on the logistics nightmare of it all, my wrists didn't feel like they were going to fall off.

When the detective returned, she released the cuffs and told me my story had checked out. "But don't skip town on me. I might have a few more questions," she said by way of parting.

"No problem. We're here through the weekend, anyway." Finn joined us and reached for my hand, but I left him hanging to massage my poor wrists. He turned his attention toward the lab techs instead. I chalked it up to morbid curiosity, but then frowning, he turned toward the detective and said, "Listen, I don't know what you're thinking, but Ziva wasn't involved in this."

"How so?"

"That woman was at least five-nine without those heels. No way Ziva could've stabbed her between the shoulders like that."

"And how tall are you, Mr. Hudson?" The detective eyed Finn over the top of her spectacles.

For the record, my beau was an even six feet. It was my turn to eye him as if to say, *Shut up!* We made our exit before either one of us could stick our feet in our mouth's again.

On the other side of the barricade, the media descended on us. We dashed back to Finn's truck, keeping our heads down and refusing to answer any of the questions they shouted to us. If this was what it was like to be famous, count me out.

3

"I'll meet you back here around noon, babe." Finn left me with a kiss on the cheek and an ice pack for my wrists before heading out the next morning. Just like back home, he was abandoning me before sunup, to go fishing. He'd met another charter captain online who'd offered to take him out. I think I mumbled something like, "Whatever," or at least that's what I heard in my head before rolling over and going back to sleep. Even though I begrudged his leaving, that had been the plan all along. It didn't seem right for Finn to have to cancel his fun just because I'd found another dead body. I could've warned him about meeting people off the internet, but who were we kidding? That was *my* luck.

A couple of hours later, I sat up and rubbed the crusts from my eyes. I formulated a plan as I showered and dressed. The first order of business was finding a chai latte. I was sure the hotel's barista could whip one up, but I knew it'd be nowhere as good as those from Sweet Thangs back home. Then, I planned to stop back by DSC headquarters for a chance at picking up my phone again. With a few strokes of a makeup brush and a little eyeliner, I was in my car and headed toward the one place I'd hoped to never have to visit again in my life.

I had no idea what to expect as I stepped back through the studio doors. I wasn't even sure if I'd be able to get in, but I was surprised to find business was back to normal, sort of. The bubbly receptionist was holding court at the front desk, while coworkers sipped coffee and scarfed down donuts—a gift from management, no doubt. The food was one of the perks of working at a TV station, and it was delicious! Maybe if all went well I'd snag one on my way out. I swirled the remnants of my latte in hand. It had done the job, but left me wanting so much more. What could I say? I was a hard woman to please.

I hadn't planned on sneaking around, but since everyone was all engrossed in the latest gossip, it was easy to side-step them and creep back toward the offices. This morning, they were unlocked and mostly deserted. The fact that it was Saturday morning and most of the workers were eating donuts out front explained a lot. I made it down the hallway and around the corner to the dressing rooms without anyone seeing me. However, when I twisted the knob to the green room's door, it wouldn't budge.

"Locked? You've got to be kidding me."

I tried a few other doors before one popped open. The gold-plated name tag on front read "Sterling Gomez." I peeked my head inside the room and saw that it was empty, except for Sterling's personal items and a rack of pressed suits hanging in the corner. I hadn't seen a need to go in until I spotted the side door. My heart rate picked up as I remembered seeing one like it in the green room. In fact, Tess had walked through a similar side door the day before when she made her infamous entrance. If my memory was accurate, it meant that the dressing rooms were connected.

With one last look around, I walked inside and softly shut the door behind me. I didn't waste any time crossing the room and entering Marissa's dressing room. Thankfully, hers was also empty, except she had even more clothes set about and enough flowers placed around the room to compete with a florist, or a funeral parlor. Flowers and I don't mix, and I hadn't taken an antihistamine that morning. I held my breath and pinched my nose as I ran across her dressing room to the adjoining door. As I yanked it open, I was happy to find the main green room. This was basically a catch-all area, which had doubled as the network's metaphorical water cooler during my visit the day before. Everyone seemed to pass through, chat for a minute, have their makeup touched up, or stop and meet a noteworthy guest.

I didn't even need to turn on the light to spot my phone, along with my hoodie, nestled on the back of the couch. I almost had my fingertips on it when the other side door popped open. I don't know why I hid. Probably because I was in a dark room, creeping around where I didn't belong, but it was a smart move. Two men entered and spoke in hushed tones. A brash, British voice rang out first. "I told you I wouldn't tolerate this." I recognized him as the huffy man Marissa had told off the day before. I didn't dare peek out from behind the couch to confirm.

A velvety voice tickled my ears next. "No, you told me not to get caught." It was Sterling. His voice was one of his best assets.

"Same difference. I'm warning you, the women might love you, but I can replace you in a snap." He clicked his fingers for emphasis.

"Don't threaten me, Rupert. It won't end well." It was silent for a beat and I suspected the men were staring each other down. The tension was thick as honey in the room. "Besides, I already told you, I'll take care of it."

"I don't want to know. Just don't screw me." *Sweet sugar!* What explosive information had I just become privy to?

The men both slipped out the side door and disappeared opposite of the way I had entered. I didn't wait long to follow suit, and planned on backtracking through Marissa's dressing room. As soon as I shut Marissa's door behind me, her front door creaked open and a shadowy figure peered in. I hit the deck for the second time that morning, army crawling the very short distance to hide in the side clothing rack, praying the person hadn't spotted me. I hugged my knees to my chest and used Marissa's heavy beaded gowns as cover. The scent of her floral perfume mixed with the lilies on the nearby table was almost too much. I covered my mouth with my hand and took shallow breaths to prevent an allergy attack.

The ominous figure slinked across the room, like a jaguar stalking its prey. If it's prey were diamonds, that is. Surely, the sparkly necklace the thief pulled from the vanity drawer couldn't have been real, but it appeared to be of real importance to whoever this was. The thief pocketed the piece and exited out the side door without a backwards glance. I sat baffled for a moment before realizing I needed to skedaddle before I witnessed any other crimes. I waited a minute to make my move. Unlike the other two visitors, I made my exit out the front door and didn't see another soul until I was back in the lobby. Everyone continued to mingle about and, I swear to goodness gracious, I felt as if I had been transferred to an alternate reality. Thankfully, I was pulled back down to Earth when I spotted a Boston Cream donut across the room. Okay, so maybe my beeline for the exit took a detour, but as soon as I had that donut, I was out of there.

I took inventory in the parking lot. Donut in one hand and my cell phone in the other? Success! Even if it had come with a heavy dose of bizarre.

My pastry was gone by the time I hopped in the driver's seat of Finn's truck, and I had no reason to worry about smearing chocolate on the leather. Now *that* would've been a crime. As I drove back to the hotel, I couldn't stop thinking about what I witnessed. This case intrigued me. How could it not? A murdered TV host, coworkers threatening one another, and a cat burglar on the payroll? I shook my head to clear it, but the curiosity didn't leave.

"Stay out of it," I said to myself. "It's not your business. Let them clear your name, then you need to head home and forget about it. You're not the police."

~

I'M PRETTY sure I repeated that same phrase all the way to the hotel until I believed it ... well, sort of. For the first time in more than twenty-four hours, I was finally able to relax. Finn would be back in about an hour and then we could get this weekend back on track, perhaps with a mid-morning tryst and then some lunch—ocean-side. Or, maybe we'd just stay between the sheets and order room service. I had to admit, option two sounded mighty appealing.

I drew an inviting bubble bath and slipped underneath the suds, letting the water wash away the stress. Of course, as soon as I managed to convince myself to let the case go, I started thinking about it once more. How was Sterling involved? I assumed he was, given what I had overheard him say to Rupert. Maybe I could somehow submit an anonymous tip? Although, how I would tell the police about a private conversation I had overheard, without outing myself, was beyond me.

The knock on the door caught me by surprise. I had planned on greeting Finn in my peach silk romper, and didn't give it another thought until I opened the door and came face-to-face with the most adorable blond-haired girl I had ever seen. She couldn't have been more than eighteen.

"Oh. I must have the wrong room. Is Finn Hudson staying here?"

I folded my arms across my chest, realizing the sheerness of my attire. "No, you've got the right room.'" I motioned to my *outfit*, "I actually thought you were him just now."

"Oh, I'm sorry. I just have some paperwork my brother asked me to drop off for him, from the marina."

"Here, come in and let me throw on something a bit more appropriate." I held the door open for the girl. She reluctantly looked around but accepted my invitation. "I'll just be a minute." I grabbed a pair of denim shorts and a tank top and quickly ducked into the bathroom. When I came back out, the girl was pretty much right where I'd left her. "He should be back any minute, if you want to wait for him," I said. I looked around for my phone thinking I'd shoot Finn a quick text about his *guest*.

"Actually, I have to get back to the docks. Would you mind giving this to him?" The girl held out an envelope. "I guess Finn missed a spot. Can you just have him sign it today and drop it back off so we can process everything?"

I had no idea what this girl was talking about, but I was not about to tell her that. "Yeah, absolutely. No problem."

"Great, thanks so much." I placed the envelope on the desk and then escorted her out.

I turned and stared at the envelope again, trying to convince myself that it was none of my business, but I failed miserably at that. By the time I walked past it for the third time in less than five seconds, I thought, *to hell with it,* and lifted the flap to peek inside. I couldn't tell much by looking at it, so I had to take it out to read it. Now, I'm no lawyer and all, but I sure know a contract when I see one. I reread the first few lines several times until I got the general gist of it. Finn had just signed a very lucrative deal to manage one of the marina's charter vessels and, judging by the date on the contract, it looked as if he was set to start immediately, in Tampa. As in a six-hour drive from Port Haven! I'm not sure which emotion I felt first. Anger? Betrayal? Or, just plain hurt that Finn hadn't trusted me enough to tell me about any of this.

I debated my options. One, I could place the contract back in the envelope, leave it on the desk as if nothing had happened, and wait to see how it played out when Finn arrived. Two, I could rip the stupid paper into a million little pieces. Even though it wouldn't make the problem go away, it would make me feel better. Three, I could snap a picture of the contract and text it to Finn, along with a couple of unpleasant emoticons. Perhaps a lovely one sporting a middle-finger gesture? Or four, and the one that I was really leaning toward, wait for Finn to arrive then have it out with him. As I paced the room, agitation built inside me, and I realized that I couldn't just sit there and wait for Finn to come back. My reaction would be nuclear. So, instead of wearing a hole in the carpet, I laced up my running shoes and hoped that a workout would cool my jets.

4

I started running without giving much thought to where I was headed. I was too mad to pay much attention to any landmarks and had zero interest in the scenery. Questions surfed through my mind like a movie reel. *What was Finn thinking? Was he even planning to tell me about this? Taking a job in Tampa ... and then what? Break up with me? Was this his plan all along?!* I had to admit, I didn't see that one coming. I thought things were good between us, really good, make that great, but I must've been mistaken. I had some commitment issues, but we were working through them. I even let Finn leave his toothbrush at my apartment, and I relinquished my top dresser drawer for his spare clothes. Okay, half of my top dresser drawer, but it was something.

I was starting to second-guess myself, heading down a path of self-depreciation, when I realized that I had jogged into a residential area. I probably wouldn't have even recognized it if I hadn't almost run straight into a toddler zipping down his driveway on a Big Wheel. The mother and I yelled "sorry" to one another at the same time, and I finally slowed somewhat to catch my breath. I was huffing and puffing harder than I wanted to admit, unsure of how much of my emotions were to blame. I really should've grabbed a water before heading out, but I was out of luck now and, by the looks of the townhouses that surrounded me, there wasn't a convenience store in sight. I turned around and started walking in the direction I hoped was back toward town, this time keeping an eye out for pedestrians, when wouldn't you know it, I spotted Claire once more. The redhead appeared to be making a hasty retreat, throwing her designer luggage into the back of a white convertible, jumping in the driver's seat, and zipping down the driveway, almost taking out a couple of skateboarders in the process. It made my near-crash with the toddler seem minor. Unlike me, Claire didn't even offer an apology as she burned rubber on the way out.

Claire's spectacle caused me to forget about Finn for a minute. The young host was skipping town. But why? What did she know about Marissa's murder or Sterling's involvement with it? I thought once again about calling the police and making them privy to the information I had garnered this morning, but I held off. I reminded myself that I didn't want to get too involved and I didn't need Detective Blackwell, the hawkish officer from the day before, to know that I had been sneaking around on set again. That opened up too many questions that I did not want to answer.

~

I PAVED a slow path back to the hotel, taking various side streets and detours until I found the boardwalk and followed it to where we were staying. I spent the time with my thoughts equally split between Marissa's murder and Finn's betrayal, both of which left an icky feeling in my stomach that I knew chocolate wouldn't fix. When I got to the hotel room, I was surprised to discover that Finn wasn't back yet. I looked at the clock and saw that it was just after 1 P.M. He was about an hour late. I checked my phone as well and was surprised that he hadn't called or texted either. I chucked the device down on the bed and sulked off to the shower. By the time I got out of the shower and saw that he still was not back, I was downright miffed. I snatched a chocolate bar out of the mini fridge, grabbed my laptop and plopped down on the bed, determined to find the answers to at least some of the questions that plagued me.

I decided to do a little bit of social media stalking to find out more about Claire, maybe even discover where she was running off to. Her Facebook profile was all professional and obviously not managed by her but probably by someone at the network. However, I struck gold when I found an old Instagram profile that she hadn't deleted.

There were hundreds of photos of her slightly younger self with friends, and most likely her family, on a beach that I knew well, very well. I would bet any money Claire's family had a vacation home in Port Haven. The striped iconic lighthouse, and the bluffs? Yeah, there was no mistaking the landscape my hometown was so famous for. Not to mention a shot of Sweet Thangs in the background, while she and her girlfriends licked ice cream cones and giggled. The photos might've been a few years old, but there were so many of them that it couldn't have just been a coincidence or a one-time vacation. Her family either had a home there or she was close to someone who did, if all the photos and check-ins were any indication. And with it being only a six-hour drive away, it was easily accessible. I filed that information away in my mind as Finn walked into the room.

I thought I was going to play it cool and give him a

chance to explain, but I erupted instead. I crossed the room, grabbed the envelope, and threw it at his chest. “What the hell is this all about?” Finn had never seen this side of me. Wide-eyed, he stared back, fumbling for an excuse.

“I, um, you see...” He may have even thrown out a curse word or two while he looked around for someone to bail him out. It only got worse. Suffice it to say, he hadn’t planned on telling me about it just yet and was shocked that I found out.

I pointed in his face. “If you think this is going down on your terms, you have another thing coming, buddy.”

“I wasn’t going to tell you.”

“Yeah, I got that. But what I don’t understand is why you’re not even giving me the courtesy of an explanation.”

“Let me finish,” Finn protested, but the words failed to come to him.

“That’s what I thought.”

The hotel room’s phone rang. I ignored it.

“You gonna get that?” Finn asked me.

“Not planning on it,” I said.

Finn marched across the room and snatched up the receiver. I thought it was a coward’s way out, and a chance to buy some time to think of an explanation. I was surprised, however, to hear him apologizing. Apparently, our argument had escalated to the point that fellow guests had called down to the front desk to complain about us. I hadn’t even realized I had been shouting, but that just goes to show you how upset I was. Finn relayed the information from the hotel staff and stared at me, waiting for my next move. I thought about yelling more, and even crying, which was not something I did often. Instead, I threw my hands up and walked out the door. It wasn’t until I was in front of the hotel without my wallet that I fully analyzed my decision. Finn had driven us down here and I wasn't about to take off with his truck, even if I had had his keys with me at that moment. All I could do was walk and maybe wait for him to leave the room before going back up to gather my things, and come up with a plan.

5

I ended up at the beach, staring at the waves and looking for a moment of serenity. The beach always seemed to calm me. I watched the rolling waves and willed myself not to cry, but it was hard because I was hurt, and angry, and once again disappointed in a man I loved. My first thought was to reach out to my best friend Aria. How we'd become and remained besties for so long was beyond me. Where she ate a mostly plant-based diet and exercised daily (usually several times), I stuck to a fat-packed diet and exercised when the guilt became too much. But she was my girl and I was hers, and there was never any doubt that we had each other's backs. In fact, if I didn't care about her so much, I would've called her that instant. But I couldn't do that to her. She was with her new blended family at Disney World, and there was no way I was going to impose on her much-needed family time. Things in that department were still not going smoothly no matter how hard she and Vince tried to make the kids get along. But I had all the confidence in the world they would find a way to make it work. Obviously, Aria had enough drama to deal with. She didn't need me to add more.

The only other person I could think to call was my dad. I knew he'd have the right words for me, but I wasn't sure I was ready to hear them yet. I wandered down the coast and found myself climbing the steps of a lifeguard tower that overlooked the frothy shore. The scenery was mesmerizing. In that moment, I promised myself I would always live near the water. I may not know anything about relationships, but I was starting to finally learn a thing or two about myself. I was one with the ocean. I belonged there.

I closed my eyes and listened to the waves, and picked up the conversation of a couple who were just down the way on the opposite side of the tower.

"You know you mean the world to me and honestly, I just can't imagine my life without you..."

Sweet sugar, you've got to be kidding me! Just my luck, I'd found the one spot on this massive beach where a proposal was happening.

"I love you. There's no other person I want to spend the rest of my life with..."

My mood dropped another notch, deluging me with all sorts of depressing feelings. I could tell when the guy dropped to one knee and opened the box, by the girl's squeal. Only a second passed before I heard a tearful-but-joyful, "Yes!"

I'd shared a few tears as well by then, for a whole different reason. I thought Finn was "the one" for me. I was sick of thinking I had found the right guy only to have my heart broken. I left the happy couple to celebrate their engagement in private and made my way back down the steps with plans to cut under the tower and back to the boardwalk.

My plans changed abruptly when I spotted the dead body floating face-down in the surf. Make that the dead body of a rich man. He had to be rich, given the expensive suit and watch he wore. His jewelry glinted in the sun. My first thought was this was no robbery, seeing that he was still in possession of his valuables. My second thought was there was no way I was calling it in. I debated what to do. I considered leaving the poor fellow and letting someone else deal with it. Heartless? Maybe, but I didn't want to think what would happen if that detective found out that I had discovered another body. I had a feeling that she didn't believe much in coincidences.

I started to backtrack and ran right into the happy couple from above. The woman screamed when she saw the body. The dead man's shoulders lifted ever so slightly with the rolling waves, marking a morbid cadence. It was the type of scene that would've freaked me out, a body or two ago. But now? Now I just rolled with it.

The fiancé's eyes went wide and he pulled his bride-to-be closer to him when he spotted the poor chap, now lying face-down in the sand. He looked from the body to me, shock clearly on his face, seemingly searching my eyes for answers. I just shrugged and blew out a puff of air. So much for pretending that I hadn't been there.

~

THE INVESTIGATION of the crime scene had gone about as well as I could have expected. I should have left. I wormed my way out of calling the body in and wanted to hightail it out of there before the police—and most likely, Detective Blackwell—arrived, but I knew she'd eventually find out that I was there. So, I waited. It seemed like the kind of thing an innocent person would do. I tried to explain that to Detective Blackwell when she arrived, but that didn't work.

"So, tell me again why I'm sitting in an interrogation room?" I asked.

"You never told me our victim embarrassed you on national TV Friday night."

"I wouldn't say *embarrassed*. It was more like she was having an off day."

"I saw the tape. It was brutal."

I grimaced at the memory, and Detective Blackwell confirmed that it was as bad as I'd imagined. I knew Finn was lying when he had said it wasn't *too bad*. Lying seemed to be a habit Finn picked up somewhere along the way. Unless it was a talent he had always possessed. I couldn't think about that jerk right now though, not with Detective Blackwell staring me down, hoping I would slip up and she'd be able to finger me for two homicides.

"Let me lay it out for you," the detective continued. "You were seen this morning going back into the building and sneaking around the offices. That behavior alone is suspicious, not to mention you're the one who called in the murder yesterday and you were present when they found Sterling's body this afternoon."

I couldn't fake the shock on my face. "Sterling? That was *his* body underneath the lifeguard tower?" I never did get a look at his face and I hadn't cared at the time to ID him. After all, what was the chance I would know him? I was on vacation, after all.

"Let's also not forget the fact that witnesses heard you and your boyfriend fighting this morning."

"We weren't fighting. It was a ... disagreement." I looked around the room, half expecting Finn to materialize, but he was nowhere to be found. I wondered if he had been brought in for questioning, or was I the only lucky one?

"Did *he* kill her? Is that what you two were fighting about?"

"What? That's absurd. Clearly, you don't know Finn Hudson at all." I reminded myself that, apparently, I didn't know him that well either, but Detective Blackwell didn't need to become privy to that little tidbit.

"Where's your boyfriend now?"

I had to admit that I had no idea. I was going to tell her that I half expected him to be in the room next door, but I didn't want to give her any ideas.

I tuned out Detective Blackwell's ranting and thought back to the conversation I had overheard this morning between Sterling and Rupert, the mystery man. What had Sterling said exactly? That he would *take care of it*. Clearly, that didn't happen. *Or did it?*

"Is there any chance it was a suicide?" The more I thought about it, the more I wondered if Sterling killed Marissa and then himself. Why, I wasn't sure. Maybe he realized he wouldn't get away with it. He was obviously involved in her murder somehow.

"Why, is that the look we're going for?" the detective asked me.

I was about to fill her in on what I had overheard, but I dropped it, thinking it would be pointless. Detective Blackwell obviously didn't think very much of me or my theories, so I kept the rest of the information to myself. Even if withholding evidence was a crime. Besides, I really wanted a chance to track down Claire and get some information out of her. I had a feeling she was a big piece of this puzzle.

6

It was almost 9 P.M. when I was finally able to leave the station. I may have willingly allowed her to question me, but that was the end of the line for my hospitality. If she wanted to talk to me again, I'd have a lawyer present. I knew the detective wanted to detain me, but she and I both knew she had nothing on me. It wasn't a crime to find two dead bodies. For me, it seemed to be more of an occupational hazard. I stood on the sidewalk outside the police station and checked my phone to see if I'd missed any calls or texts from Finn, but I hadn't. His silence surprised me and left me more angry than I'd ever admit. I looked up and down the street and plotted my next move. I had a feeling Detective Blackwell would be a permanent fixture in my life until she had another suspect to focus on. Therefore, my plan was to find her another suspect, perhaps even the real killer. I needed to talk to Claire. Besides, I much preferred working on solving a murder, make that a double murder, over dealing with my personal life in that moment.

I used the app on my phone to call for an Uber and

waited for him to come take me to the airport. Detective Blackwell would have a field day if she thought I was skipping town, but I wasn't. Not really. I was just going back home, and she knew where to find me. I thought for a second about taking a flight back as opposed to driving, but who was I kidding? I wasn't about to board any aircraft without my Xanax prescription. Flying was not my favorite thing to do, unless it was on Aria's husband's private jet. *That* I could manage. For now, I opted to rent a car.

It was about a six-hour drive from Tampa to Port Haven, one I didn't mind making solo this time. There was no way in hell I was about to ride across town with Finn, much less across state lines. It was probably smart of Finn to avoid me right now because, I swear, if he were anywhere near my car, I might've accidentally swerved and run his butt over. Okay, okay, I wouldn't do that, especially since *his butt* was a pretty darn nice one. Still, I was in no mood to deal with Finn Hudson anytime soon.

As the hours slipped by, so did my resolve. My eyes glistened with tears threatening to spill over my cheeks. I wasn't sure how much longer I could swallow them back. I blamed my mood entirely on sleep deprivation and the depressing music that filled my car. I was only one country song away from becoming a hot mess.

How did I let this happen? Of course, I knew the answer. Finn was my perfect neighbor. A genuine good guy with a knack for fixing things, most of the time without his shirt on, which may have sped the process of me approaching him. He was the kind of man a girl dreamed about meeting. I never realized that before, or maybe I just never admitted it before. Regardless, all of that was total rubbish now. But why? What had happened? How had I not seen this coming? Those questions plagued me for the duration of my drive. I wasn't sure what my next steps were or how I was going to move on from this. Finn's deceit ripped my heart open. Being ever the optimist, I told myself this could be a good thing. I'd never been good at commitment, and it had taken me a long time to come around to Finn being a permanent staple in my life. Now I was free of him, free to put the focus on myself and my business again. As rapidly as Sugar & Sass was growing, I'd have plenty to keep me busy. Who had time for a boyfriend anyway?

I'd almost convinced myself that I was better off without him, until one tear slipped loose. Then it was game over.

I'm not a cute crier. I'm more of a sloppy-ugly-crocodile-tears crier. Add raccoon-faced crier to that, seeing I hadn't worn *waterproof* mascara. When the hiccupping began, I had to pull over at a rest stop and blow my nose.

"Stupid! Stupid! Man!" I smacked the steering wheel with each word. In fact, I would have choked the steering wheel if I had thought it would make me feel better. I may have even growled a time or two. "Don't do this to yourself," I rationalized aloud. But the tears didn't get the message until much later. In hindsight, it was good I had taken this drive alone. The wee morning hours gave me plenty of time to sort out a few things; although, finally realizing how in love with Finn I was did me no good, since he was about to break up with me.

I guess if anything, I can say I learned a bit more about myself. Let's hear it for self-reflection. I filed that thought away for personal growth and reminded myself to pat me on the back later.

BY THE TIME I made it back to Port Haven, I was pretty sure I was dehydrated. My mood had finally lifted about the time I changed the radio station and crossed the Georgia/South Carolina border.

It was almost 4 A.M. when I pulled into the gravel alley behind my apartment and parked the little Ford Focus next to my cute little pickup truck. I smacked the hood of my truck as a way of greeting and wished that I had driven down to Tampa in the first place. At least I avoided some wear and tear on it.

I had no luggage to gather from the rental car, since all my stuff was still back at the hotel with Finn, where it could stay as far as I was concerned. I climbed my apartment's back steps and went straight inside to my bedroom and crawled into bed, not bothering to put on pajamas or wash my face. This was one great benefit to using all-natural makeup—it didn't clog my pores. I would have no regrets about my skin in the morning, and my sheets would still be clean, not covered in paraben pigments. I would never tell my Beauty Secrets clients, but little by little, I had replaced my stash of Beauty Secrets products with my own creations, and my skin had never looked better.

It was after 10 A.M. when I opened my eyes again in a panic. My first thought was of Captain Jack, my beloved fluffy white poodle. I had forgotten he was at Inez's house and not waiting for me to let him out. Inez was Aria's grandmother-in-law and she loved Captain Jack as much as I did. The little fur ball. He would've had a fit if I had slept in that long and didn't let him out for his morning piddle and bowl full of kibble. I was becoming a big sap because, man, I sure did miss the little guy. *All the more reason to get down to business and catch a killer*, I thought as I stretched to wake my muscles. I got ready as quickly as my addled brain would allow me to, and focused my energy on tracking down Claire.

Standing outside, I surveyed my ride options. I preferred my truck over the rental car, but I thought it might make more sense to go incognito for a bit. Claire had no idea what I drove, but since the rental car wasn't due back until later that afternoon, I figured I might as well take advantage of it.

My first mistake of the day was getting the mail before heading out. My second mistake was opening the thick ivory envelope. I pulled out the invitation, not even bothering to read the return address, and felt all the air escape my lungs. Justine and Todd were getting married. Justine, as in my former arch enemy, who I had recently made nice with; and Todd, my former fiancé, who cheated on me with the cocktail waitress. Those two, ugh. I took in a shaky breath and reminded myself that I was supposed to be happy for them. But I wasn't.

What was this? Justine's sixth, maybe seventh, marriage? She had never felt compelled to invite me to one of her weddings before, so why start now? If she was a nice person, one could surmise that maybe she had returned my offer of friendship by extending an olive branch, but she wasn't a nice person. Knowing Justine, she probably took this as an opportunity to gloat about her success at marrying my ex. Although, I had to admit, I was happy she was the one marrying him, and not me. I've said it once and I'll say it again, my nana really saved me on that one. As a matter of fact, I had kept my guardian angel very busy these last few months. I reached up to touch the cross around my neck and sighed.

I dropped the invitation in my bag, next to a king-sized candy bar, a pair of oversized shades, my water bottle, sunscreen, and a well-worn romance novel. This wasn't my first stakeout. I knew the afternoon could be long, and the sun was hot. I opened the rental car's back door to throw in my bag and was shocked at the number of candy wrappers scattered across the backseat. One might be surprised how many of those fun-sized bars can be consumed during a six-hour road trip. I collected the wrappers and balled them into a giant wad of tinfoil, and threw them in the outside trash can. Normally, I probably would have admonished myself for all the calories I had consumed the night before, but what did it matter anymore? I had no one to impress. With that last thought in mind, I hopped in the car and headed over to Sweet Thangs to get my beloved child latte, a venti with extra sprinkles, and maybe even a cinnamon roll. Their cream cheese icing was sweet-tooth heaven. Once I finished my gooey treat, I set out to track down Claire. This girl was going to do some talking.

7

God bless millennials and their love of checking in everywhere. Claire's Instagram account was a treasure trove of information, even if it was a little out of date. Just by scrolling through her feed, I could see her favorite restaurants, beaches, and boutiques. It seemed she took a picture of everything she ate and every time she hit the sand or tried on clothes. I had planned on scouting the residential areas around her favorite check-ins in search of her white convertible. A couple of pictures were taken in someone's backyard, quite possibly her own, but there wasn't enough detail for me to make out anything specific. Down here, the houses seemed to blend in with one another. Each homeowner's association had an approved list of paint colors. All you had to do was pop in at the local hardware store and they'd be able to look up your plantation and let you know the acceptable colors to paint the exterior of your home. While that created a very coherent look, it made it difficult to single out one particular house. Besides that, even if I had found the picture of the house, I would never be able to match it based on color alone. Claire seemed to use filters on all her photos, altering the true color and making the matching process darn near impossible.

I wasted a little over an hour zig-zagging up and down the various subdivisions, searching for her car. It was completely pointless. Even if Claire was in Port Haven, there was a good chance she parked inside a garage or wasn't even home. It seemed like a good plan, but it didn't pan out. For all I knew, Claire had driven someplace out west, or heck, even further south to The Keys. I wouldn't mind looking for her down there next, seeing how my vacation was a bust.

And then I had an epiphany: Maybe Claire hadn't quit using Instagram because she was almost famous. Maybe she preferred a different platform. With that thought in mind, I detoured to my favorite hole-in-the-wall Chinese joint to grab lunch and do a little research. While munching on some fried pot stickers and waiting for my Singapore Noodles to come out, I thought my theory through. Facebook and Instagram were old-school, but Snapchat wasn't. I quickly downloaded the popular photo-and-video-sharing app that all the cool kids were using (notice I said I had to download it) and then I tried to find her. I didn't have her phone number (wouldn't that have been nice), so I couldn't add her based on my contact list, but I did allow the app to search through my contacts anyway and discovered that I was way behind the times. *My dad* even had an account, complete with a bitmoji cartoon character that had an uncanny resemblance. How did he even know how to do that? I thought maybe he could give me a hand tracking her down if I came up empty. Next, I tried searching for her by name, but she hadn't gone with her full name as her username, and it wasn't the same as her Instagram one either. She also hadn't posted her "Snapchat code" anywhere for me to scan, but I did find Chris Pratt's. I saved that one to my camera roll for later.

My last option was to add friends nearby, but unless I wanted to be friends with Mr. Hang, I was out of luck. Mr. Hang's daughter, however, was a different story. She brought out my steaming plate of spicy noodles and sat across from me. To say that I was a regular here was an understatement.

"Okay, you're driving me crazy here. What's up?" Lian asked.

"What do you know about Snapchat?" I was pinching my phone screen, trying to see how the map function worked, but I wasn't getting very far. I used to think I was tech savvy. Now I felt totally incompetent.

Lian had her phone out and the app open in a hot second. "Here, swipe down and then click on Add Friends and then on Nearby. I'll do the same and then I'll add you."

Sure enough, Lian and I were now following one another.

"How do I find someone?"

"I usually go through my contacts, or just share my username or code with someone."

"Any way to find someone if you don't have that info?"

Her eyes narrowed. "Who are you stalking?"

I was in the middle of taking a bite of noodles when she asked and ended up inhaling a shrimp in surprise.

"Are you okay?" Lian stood up and was ready to give me the Heimlich maneuver, but I finally coughed it up.

"Sorry," I said in broken breaths. I cleared my throat.

"Is Finn up to something shady?"

"What?! No, he's not even on the app." I double-checked by doing a quick search for his Instagram username and stared in shock when a Snapchat account popped up for him.

Lian's lips formed an O and she looked away.

"Okay, that's beside the point. He's not who I'm looking for."

"Sorry, but that's pretty much all I can think of."

"What about the map?"

"Oh, yeah. You can look for other people on the map. See how it's glowing blue over here? That shows there's been some recent Snap activity. Then see how this is glowing red by the volleyball courts? That shows there's a ton of activity; it's a hot spot, which makes sense with the tournament going down."

Mixed in with the glowing orbs were little cartoon bitmojis here and there. "These are your friends?" I asked, referencing the bitmojis.

"Yeah, or just people who've shared their location."

I copied Lian and brought up the map, looking around. *Bingo!* Claire's little red-haired bitmoji, Clairbear21, was right there on the Snap Map. I touched the bitmoji to make sure that it was in fact her. Sure enough, a video of her loaded. "All right, here's a look at the tournament. Isn't it gorgeous out today?" Claire did a panorama of the nets and the players taking to the sand. The ocean was just visible in the background. "I'm going to be out here for a couple of hours, so hit me up." I felt like I had won the lottery.

"Oh my goodness, girl, you are a lifesaver. Can I get this to go?"

"What? Oh, yeah sure." Lian jumped up and got a to-go carton. I slapped a twenty on the table and headed to the beach. I hadn't brought a bathing suit, but a quick stop at one of the beachside boutiques would remedy that. A girl could never have too many bathing suits.

I PRETENDED it was a total coincidence that I had run into her, and that I wasn't a total stalker. I thought I was quite believable.

"Oh my goodness, Claire? Is that you?" I lowered my sunglasses and peered down at the young host.

Claire was stretched out on her beach blanket, watching the men's volleyball game just in the distance. I may have been in a hater mood when it came to men, but I could still appreciate the view. Bare-chested sun gods wearing board shorts? Yes, please.

"Ziva? Hey, how's it going?" Claire rolled over on her beach towel from her belly to her back, and sat up. "You on vacation?"

"No, actually, I live here."

"You do?"

"Yeah, but no one would blame me for taking off after Friday's on-air fiasco."

"I know. Gosh, that was awful. I'm so sorry she did that to you."

"Me too."

Claire scooched over and motioned for me to lay my towel down. There wasn't a lot of space, as fans were starting to crowd in, and I knew the beach would soon be packed. I joined her in the sand and started lathering up.

"Yours?" Claire motioned to the un-labeled bottle that I was squirting lotion out of.

"You know it. I'm not a fan of commercial sunscreens for so many reasons."

Claire tilted her head in confusion.

"It has a lot of toxic chemicals, not to mention the havoc it wreaks on ocean life."

"Wow, I didn't know that."

"Yeah, so once I really got my beauty business going, I

started considering other products that needed revamping. Sunscreen became a top priority. I'm hoping it will be ready within the next few months."

"Mind if I try it?"

"Of course not, help yourself." I passed the bottle her way. "You know, I have a VIP club. You can sign up on the store's website to get free samples, if you're interested."

"I'm already a member." Claire blushed. *I knew I liked her.* I had been right in my initial assessment: Claire was a sweet girl. I noticed, now that we weren't on set, her voice had a little bit of a southern twang to it, which I pointed out to her, in a polite way, of course. "Where are you from originally?"

"Kentucky. Can y'all tell?" Claire kicked the twang up a notch.

"Just a bit," I said with a smile. "I think it's adorable, that is, if you don't find that offensive."

"No, not at all. Personally, I wish I didn't have to lose it to be on TV, but I guess you could call it an occupational hazard."

"They made you fake your accent?" I guess I was a bit more naïve than I thought when it came to the entertainment industry.

"No one asked me to directly, but you're not going to make it too far when you sound like a hillbilly, or so they told me."

"That's horrible. I never even thought of it that way." I pondered all the national television news shows and programming that I occasionally tuned into and I had to admit, I'd never heard much diversity in accents. I could see now it wasn't a coincidence.

"I heard about Marissa," I said, waiting to see how Claire would react.

She didn't even flinch. "Honestly, and I know this going to sound horrible, but it doesn't surprise me. She wasn't a very nice person. I might've not known her for that long, but I can tell you that a lot of people wanted her dead."

"I could believe that. I hardly knew her, but I could see how some people would have it in for her."

"I probably shouldn't have taken off, but the whole thing creeped me out. I know once the police start digging into her background, they're going to come to me for questioning." Shock registered on my face, without my consent, at those words. "Let's just say we didn't get along very well, and everyone knew it," Claire supplied.

"A little behind-the-scenes rivalry?"

"More than a little bit. Marissa and I were hired at the same time and even though they never said it, we knew we were competing for air time. Every time we did a segment, it was basically an on-camera audition."

"That's stressful."

"It was, absolutely. We were vying for air time for months, which is why I thought it would've been better if we were friends. Unfortunately, Marissa thought it was okay to stab her friends in the back."

"And now, someone literally did just that."

"I know."

"You said a lot of other people wanted her dead. Who else can you think of?"

"Her husband? Or I guess he's her soon-to-be ex-husband."

"She was going through a divorce?"

"A nasty one. And her husband wasn't the type of guy who liked being cast aside."

Who does? It was a bit of a dumb statement, but I continued playing into Claire's words, seeing that she looked like she wanted to spill a secret. "Really? You have to tell me about him now."

"Dr. Stewart? I guess you wouldn't know of him, being from out of town and all." She was right. I had never heard of him. "You could say he's the top plastic surgeon in all of Southern Florida, and that's saying something."

It was totally snippy of me to even wander onto this train of thought, but I could see Marissa having some work done. I shifted subtly to reinvest my attention in our conversation.

"So, the prestigious doctor's wife left him as soon as she hit the big time?" I said.

"Pretty much."

"Nice, and now there are two hosts who have been murdered."

"Wait, what?" Claire's eyes got all buggy.

"Sterling."

"Sterling's dead?" Genuine shock registered on her face.

I took advantage of the situation. "And I saw you yesterday making a run for it."

"I—I... Wait, you followed me?"

"Not at all." *I stalked you. There's a difference.* "Remember, I live here, but I have been wanting to talk to you." I gave Claire a moment to think and when she still wasn't talking, I followed it up with, "I haven't told anyone yet, but I can give the police a call and tell them what I saw, unless you'd rather?" I looked Claire in the eye so she knew I meant business.

"Fine, I know I shouldn't have run, but I panicked. Mr. Aldrich? Well, he was very angry the last time I saw him. I just assumed the worst."

"Who's he?"

"Rupert Aldrich?" Claire looked at me like I was a simpleton. "DSC's CEO?"

"Ah, that Mr. Aldrich. I can see why you'd want to get out of town for a bit."

"I thought DSC was my dream job, and now I'm not so sure. Even if this all plays out okay, the work environment is just so toxic." With the CEO going around threatening employees and possibly covering up a murder? Yeah, I could see that.

"What did he say exactly?" I thought back to his conversation with Sterling and wondered if he had also threatened Claire. "Did he approach you about anything?"

"I shouldn't be telling anyone. I'm sorry. Forget what I said." Claire looked around as if checking for anyone who had overheard our conversation.

I dropped my voice in response. "At least tell the police, seriously. Regardless if he's your boss or not."

Claire had the most cynical expression on her face. "You don't understand how this industry works. I'm not about to get black-balled when my career is just taking off. If I walk away, it's going to be on my terms, and not because I caused a scandal. I'm sorry, but I've got to go." Claire snatched up her towel, sending a cloud of sand in my direction. I shielded my eyes and let her walk away.

I lay on the beach for a little while longer and absorbed what I'd just learned. Thinking back on the conversation with Claire, I felt that her responses were genuine and that she definitely didn't kill Sterling, probably not Marissa either. Even if she did really want the job, and Marissa was as horrible to her as she had claimed. Maybe it was a whole southern belle thing, but it seemed Claire had a strong moral compass.

I could've stayed on the beach all afternoon, and debated doing so, but eventually my work ethic kicked in and I felt the need to stop by my store before picking the detective trail back up again. Of course, this had nothing to do with the fact that Finn still hadn't called or texted me. I was about to pack up when I looked over my shoulder and swore I saw Cee Cee Thomas not more than fifty feet behind me. Maybe it was a total coincidence. Maybe the entertainment reporter was covering the pro volleyball tournament. Or maybe, the woman was as eager as I was to solve this case. I could've approached her right then and there to ask, but if I was totally wrong, I didn't want to give her any ideas. Although, she could be a source of information down the road. She knew the ins and outs of Hollywood far more than I did. I pretended that I hadn't marked her and took a couple of extra minutes before packing up and leaving. She never approached me and I considered that a good thing, for now.

8

I popped into the store and found Izzy rearranging the front display. I smiled, thankful for her creative spirit. She had a knack for design, so I had no problem leaving the task to her. In fact, she had a way with a lot of things, a gift she attributed to her psychic intuition. I personally thought she was just a people-person. Much like the way she designed the layout of the store, Izzy's look and style were all her own. Her curls? Natural. The black hair color? Not so much. And her lavender-colored eyes were something out of a novel. Somedays, I'd swear her eyes were blue. Other days, they were gray. But most of the time, they were lavender and completely natural. Some people wore mood rings, but Izzy didn't have to. I could tell her feelings just by looking at her eyes and, right now, they were a stormy gray.

She whisked over to me and wrapped me in a giant hug. "Sweetie, I have no idea what happened to you, but your aura is all murky." She held me at arm's length to confirm. I looked down at my hand and saw the same tanned skin as always. "And the look on your face? Well, you have me feeling downright depressed. You need to sit down." I insisted that I was perfectly fine, but Izzy wouldn't hear it. She led me back to my office and ordered me to take a seat at my desk. I heard Izzy holler out to Margaret to hold down the fort and come find her if she needed anything. She turned to me with a raised brow. "Now, spill it."

I had no idea where to start, but I knew it would do me no good to lie. I wasn't sure how much I believed in the whole psychic-intuition bit, but nothing got past Izzy. I sighed and it all came tumbling out, seemingly as one long sentence. "Girl, I don't even believe it, but somehow I found myself smack dab in another murder investigation. And to top it off, I found out Finn is taking a job in Tampa, and he wasn't even going to tell me about it."

"He did not."

"He did. I drove back from Tampa by myself last night, in a rental car, and spent my morning interviewing a murder suspect. Speaking of the car, can you help me return it later?"

"Consider it done."

"Okay, so why aren't you freaking out with me?"

"Well, I may have seen this all coming. Sort of. When I looked at your chart last week, I saw you were headed into some relationship drama, but it looked like it would clear up on its own."

"So, you thought it best not to tell me?"

"Right. I didn't think you wanted me all up in your personal business. You only asked me to keep an eye on your professional business." She circled her hand out and around in presentation of the store.

"And the dead bodies?"

"That part I did not see coming. You somehow managed

to defy the cosmos, but honestly, I'm not surprised with you being you."

"Gee thanks," I said, and then I thought about something. "Is there some type of exorcism or something I can do to get rid of this morbid quirk I've picked up?"

"Hmm, good question. Let me look into it." I knew if anyone could find a way to right my karma, it would be Izzy.

"Thanks. Until then, I think I need to head back to Tampa to sort out a few things," I said.

"Go for it. I've got everything under control here. The store's doing fabulous, and Margaret and I can manage it another day or two."

"Thanks, girl. You're an absolute life saver." Izzy's eyes softened a little. They weren't quite lavender yet, but the storm had blown over.

"As for you and Finn? Don't worry about it."

I started to protest.

"No, let me tell you, Mercury is retrograde. All areas of your life get a little wacky when that happens, especially communication. I bet all that you have here is a communication issue." *Hmm, I thought all I had here was a deceitful boyfriend.*

"I'm serious. Last time Mercury was retrograde, I tried setting up a wire transfer to London and it ended up in Bangkok." I raised my eyebrows at that. Izzy shrugged her shoulders. "Gotta love Mercury."

"Indeed."

"Here, hang on just a second. Izzy grabbed her purse off my door's back hook and fished around inside, retrieving a smooth pink stone. "Take this." She pushed the palm-sized crystal into my hand and closed my fingers over it. I could've sworn I felt the little bugger vibrating in my hand. "This will make you feel better, raise your energy a bit. Maybe even give you a little more clarity." I put the stone in my pocket and had to admit that I did feel a bit better. Whether that was all in my head or not was yet to be determined.

"Thanks, girlie." I gave my New Age friend a hug and prepared to leave. "Oh, and by the way, when does Mercury right itself again, or do whatever it's supposed to do?"

"About a week and a half."

I wrinkled my nose. I was hoping it was more of a 24-hour thing.

~

I DROVE BACK HOME MOSTLY in a daze, and I don't think it had anything to do with the murder investigation or Finn, but more due to utter exhaustion. The drive from the night before, paired with my basking in the sun, had drained me. I thought I could grab a few winks once I got back home, but it wasn't happening. I lay on my bed, wide awake, staring at the ceiling as the wheels in my head spun wildly. I grabbed my phone off my nightstand and opened the note-taking app and started making a list of suspects. I didn't know anything about Marissa's family or her past, other than she'd been planning to get a divorce. I put "divorce" in bold, deciding that angle warranted some serious investigating. I also didn't know anything about Sterling, other than he had an impressive on-air career. Next to his name, I typed "family?" "spouse?" "friends?" and wondered who I could contact for more information on those matters.

Finally, there was good old Tess. I prayed Detective Blackwell was considering her. Last I'd seen, she was two sheets to the wind, or maybe I should say two martinis to the wind. What could've caused the Queen of the Daytime Shopping Channel to fall off her throne? I wrote the answer next to it: "Marissa and Claire." Tess had to be feeling some pressure with the new girls being brought on board. If Marissa was about to take over the prime-time segment and bring an end to Tess's reign, that sure gave Tess one heck of a motive to kill her. And if that was the case, Claire should be looking over her shoulder as well. I probably would've gotten out of town too.

Then I wrote: "charity gala." How many people had been invited? How could I get a peek at the guest list? I wrote Cee Cee's name next to it. She would probably know or could find out. Tess had been there. I'd seen her in that shiny red number. So had Sterling, Claire, Skip the Producer, and all of their dates. I wondered if Marissa's husband was also present. Yet another question Cee Cee would know.

Next, I questioned what time Marissa had been murdered. I was certain the police had an estimated time of death, fat chance of them sharing that with me though. Knowing that answer would tell me whether the gala had kicked off yet, and if all the guests were, in fact, suspects. Any one of them could have murdered her, or none of them at all, but rather someone who used the event as a distraction to sneak in, much like I did. Security had been lax, for sure. I never saw anyone of authority until I called the police.

I thought more about how Marissa had been murdered—stabbed in the back—and pondered its significance. Had the killer been trying to send a message? One thing I knew for sure, it took a lot of anger to stab someone to death. I had a feeling this wasn't a premeditated murder, not with the fact that she'd been killed with an object that was left on set. No, this seemed to me like a crime of passion, which brought me back to her husband, and possibly even Tess.

I closed my eyes and pictured the details of the scene. I

didn't recall seeing any signs of struggle. Nothing had been broken—no overturned tables, or anything of that nature. Her up-do was smooth and her dress was flawless. What's more, Marissa still had her heels on. If she had fought or tried to run, one or both of her heels would've come off in the chaos. I'd almost bet money that there had been a confrontation and she turned her back on her attacker, never suspecting harm.

I reminded myself that I needed to get back to Tampa if I was going to answer any of these questions. I took my extra overnight tote from the closet and quickly stuffed in a couple of pairs of shorts, a few tees, and a pair of pajamas. I raided my bathroom drawers for some extra cleanser, moisturizer, and a lipstick. That would have to be good enough for now. The rest of my beauty arsenal was still back at the hotel room with Finn. Even if I didn't want to talk to him about our relationship status, I did need to get my stuff back. Once I was all packed up, I called Inez. She was more than willing to keep my little guy for a few more nights. I promised her I'd be back in town by Wednesday at the latest. She might not have minded keeping him longer, but I really did miss my little puppy.

9

This time my solo road trip was tear-free. I was on a mission. I'd chosen a new hotel based upon its room service choices listed online. Of course, I had to drive by my previous hotel to see if Finn's truck was parked there. It wasn't. "Guess you must be out celebrating your new windfall," I said to myself, gripping the steering wheel a bit too tight. I decided I might need to do some yoga before going to bed that night. I was sure Aria would have all sorts of meditation advice if I were to call her. Sitting still and quiet wasn't really my strong suit, but perhaps I needed to try.

I pulled into my new hotel and gave an inward smile. It looked perfect. Although, I'm not sure *hotel* was the right word to describe it. It was luxury personified. I couldn't wait to escape to my room, make that—suite, which promised to "indulge my senses and renew my soul." Yes, please.

I walked into the South Tampa retreat and relaxed almost instantly. I preferred my home a little shabby chic, but I enjoyed this hotel's twist on urban contemporary style.

As I crossed the hotel lobby, I came to a dead stop. Right

there in the spa's front window were my products. Sugar & Sass was front and center, and boy did she look pretty. Now *that* made me smile. My little business sure was making a name for itself. I knew Izzy had been working on securing new contracts and product placements, and I chose to leave that to her. Like I said, she was a real people-person and people seemed eager to please her in return. We'd sent out a few samples to some local spas and they were hooked right away. I had lost count of how many product placements we had garnered in the last couple of months, but I knew I had earned enough money to pay back my original investment backer. Not that she was too keen to accept the payment. Mrs. DeVine was a wealthy woman for a reason. She knew my business was about to explode, and she was thrilled to remain a part of it. I was fine with that, and very appreciative for her initial loan, but I wanted the terms to have a more even footing, which is why I retained 85% ownership, leaving her a small slice of the pie.

My suite was everything it promised to be, and after plopping down on the super soft bed and watching the flat-screen television raise and lower out of the dresser a few dozen times, I was downright bored. *Relax!* I told myself. *Order up some room service, binge watch Gilmore Girls.* But I knew that if I ordered room service, the only thing I would've ended up binging on was ice cream, especially if they had mint chocolate chip. As it was, I was pretty sick of being alone all day in the car. After checking my phone and still no word from Finn, I decided to scope out the hotel bar instead.

Wouldn't you know it, Ms. Tess herself was seated front and center at the long glass bar. What's more, even from across the room I could tell she already had a couple of drinks in her. Either that, or she always leaned a little to the left when sitting on a bar stool. I took a seat next to her and ordered a chocolate martini. No reason to skip on dessert entirely.

"I know you," I said to her when the bartender walked away. "You're Ms. Hill. I'm a huge fan."

"You are?" Tess perked right up.

"Absolutely. I love watching your jewelry segments."

"Yes, that's my favorite too. What's your name, dear?"

I could've lied and given her a fake name, but I didn't feel the need to. "Ziva, Ziva Diaz. I own Sugar & Sass Skincare."

"I love your moisturizer."

"Thank you so much."

"Weren't you just on the show?"

I was surprised she remembered me, seeing she'd completely disregarded me on Friday.

"I was. That was a bit of a disaster."

"That whole place is a disaster."

I took the opening. "I heard big changes were in store at DSC."

"Don't remind me." Tess lifted her finger to signal another drink. I was surprised when the bartender started making her another one. One would think he would have cut her off. "Let me tell you about that place. They see me as washed up, but I'm still in my prime."

"I don't doubt it."

Tess ignored my compliment. "I've done everything for them. I've been injected, plumped, and pruned. Given them the best years of my life, and this is how they treat me?"

"It's disgusting."

"It is and what's worse... Sterling was going to get to stay. The jerk." The bartender set our drinks in front of us. Tess slid the olive off the toothpick with her lips and followed it up with a big gulp of her drink. When she looked up at me, her eyes were a bit crossed. "Don't think I didn't see it coming, but I thought I had more time. A few more years. The network's doing me *the honor* of hosting an on-air farewell party for me. Did you hear that? They're calling it a surprise. Of course, I know all about it. As if that makes it okay that they're kicking me out after being a part of the show for thirty years. *Early-retirement*, that's what Mr. Aldrich called it. Said I should be living it up in my golden years. I'll show them *my golden years*."

It was obvious that Tess was hurt and angry, feelings I knew well, especially as of late.

"Did you hear about Sterling?" I asked.

Tess actually snorted and I thought for a second she might've accidentally inhaled an olive down the wrong pipe. "That fool. That blonde bimbo of his warped his mind." I had no idea who she was talking about, but I had a feeling it wasn't his wife, and I said as much. "His wife? Good heavens, no. MJ might be a little plain, but she was loyal and she loved Sterling. No, I'm talking about Sterling hooking up with Marissa."

My voice elevated an octave. "Say what?"

"Let me just tell you, they shouldn't have been doing the dirty in his dressing room. Those walls are paper thin. And I thought she was my protégé." Tess snorted again and I hoped she'd skip the sound effects. She obviously wasn't that upset about her long-time co-host's death or Marissa's.

"And Marissa? That girl could scream." I so did not need to hear this. "Don't give me that look, that's not what I'm talking about. A couple of days ago, I was waiting outside Mr. Aldrich's office for a personal meeting when I heard her screaming and shouting on the other side. Apparently, she wasn't happy about something. Of course, at the time, I'm sitting there all smug thinking I'm still on top. Little did I know I was about to get fired. Oh wait, I'm sorry. What did I say he called it? Oh yes, *early retirement*."

I had to say that if Mr. Aldrich was ever found murdered, I'd know who did it. Tess was seething. "Any theory as to what happened?"

"Oh, I'll give you a theory. Little Miss Blondie called off her relationship with Sterling and he went off the deep end. I'll bet he killed her and then himself. Simple as that." Tess lifted her finger for another cocktail.

No, I thought, it was never as simple as that. But at least Tess gave me a theory to work from, and it was very similar to the one that I had already formulated.

~

I DIDN'T FEEL comfortable leaving Tess sitting there all vulnerable at the bar, but she insisted that Mitch, the bartender, would assure she made it home. It took me a minute, but I finally realized that she lived upstairs in the penthouse and it appeared to be a pretty common trend for her to sit at the bar and drink away her sorrows, at least recently anyhow. Mitch nodded that he would see to it, though he didn't look all that thrilled about the prospect.

Back upstairs, I thought about it some more. Could the whole murder-suicide story be right? Was that Sterling's way of *taking care of things* and telling Mr. Aldrich not to worry about it? I was no longer sure. I needed to talk to more people—specifically Mr. Aldrich, Marissa's husband, Dr. Stewart; and Sterling's wife, Mary Jane.

In truth, there were too many questions for me to answer. It was better that I realized that then, instead of driving myself crazy trying to track all the details down. So, I took a chance and reached out to Cee Cee Williams. I did a quick search on her credentials and she seemed like a legitimate reporter given her journalism degree and past editorial work. I used the contact form listed on her network site and shot off a quick email, making sure to mention who I was and how I was connected to the case, in hopes of a quick reply. Hopefully, she'd have some answers. The media always seemed to get the inside scoop, and that is exactly what I needed. Detective Blackwell was not going to be sharing any information with me and if Cee Cee didn't have the answers, we would just have to work together. Divide and conquer.

10

I wasn't ready for Monday morning and even more so once I remembered where I was and what I was trying to do—solve a double homicide. I really should have been getting paid for my investigative skills.

Today was also the day that Finn and I were scheduled to leave town. I wondered if he would call me or assume that I'd already made other arrangements. My phone rang on the bedside table and I'm embarrassed to say I jumped for it, eager to see if it was Finn calling to make amends. I answered the phone and hoped I didn't sound as bummed out as I felt. "Morning, Izzy, how's it going there?"

"Forget that, love. How's it going for you?"

"I've been better."

"Well, I just wanted to give you a heads-up. I ran your chart last night and, let's just say, you'd better keep your wits about you. Try to stay out of trouble. You need to be careful, don't trust people so much." Of course, I thought of Finn. It was a little too late for that warning.

"Okay, got it." Try not to get killed or have your heart broken. "How's the store doing?"

"Awesome. I entered the new figures into the books, so go ahead and check out the link. I emailed it to you last night. Let me know if you have any questions."

"Sales been okay?"

"Okay? They're fabulous. You know what they say, there's no such thing as bad publicity."

"Seriously?"

"Swear it. In fact, we're running low on inventory."

"Got it." Looked like I had a ton of computer work to do. Even with Izzy running the store, there were still a lot of behind-the-scenes tasks to manage. No vacations for true business owners, I supposed.

"Hey, there's something else I wanted to talk to you about, and we can get into the details when you get back, but I was wondering what you thought about hiring someone to manage the online store? Maybe even part-time?"

I closed my eyes and pictured it. We needed the extra help, even though I hadn't planned on bringing anyone else on board yet. The online store was a full-time job on its own. "No, that's a promising idea. I'll create a job posting and send it to you to look over. I'll be back in a couple of days. In the meantime, keep sending me the daily inventory and sales figures, and I'll make sure to log on and let you know if I have any questions."

"Got it."

"And Izzy? You're a lifesaver." I meant that in more ways than one.

I checked the email from Izzy. *That girl sure is efficient.* My mouth dropped when I saw the weekend's revenue totals. "Wowzers. She wasn't kidding." *My nest egg just became a lot bigger.* I had dollar signs dancing in my eyes, and that desire from Friday night to go shopping hit me once more.

I also had an email from Cee Cee: *Hey, Ziva, I'd love to meet up. Tonight okay? Say 8 P.M. at Dockside?*

I sent a reply to confirm the time and got ready for the day with more enthusiasm than I had thought possible. With Cee Cee and I working together, I had a feeling we'd crack this case wide open.

~

MAYBE IT WAS the quartz crystal humming in my pocket, or maybe it was because I finally felt like I was getting somewhere with this case. Whatever the cause, I took my newfound optimism with me back to DSC headquarters to get some answers. Yes, I was taking a huge risk going back to the studio, but I wanted to chat with Mr. Aldrich before meeting Cee Cee tonight, and the studio was my best chance at seeing him.

Instead of trying to sneak around and bypass the receptionist, I put on my megawatt smile that said, "*I'm confident!*" and walked right up to her desk.

"Hi, Jenny. I don't know if you remember me, but my name is Ziva Diaz."

The receptionist's wide-eyed expression told me she knew exactly who I was. "Yes, *that* Ziva Diaz," I confirmed.

"Oh my word, I can't believe you found Marissa's body. I would've totally freaked out and had a heart attack right there."

"It was pretty scary," I replied, making sure my continuance was reflected in my expression. "And now Sterling?" I raised my eyebrows. Jenny lowered her voice and leaned forward. "They were having an affair, you know?"

"They were not!" Jenny nodded her head. I leaned in and lowered my voice to match hers, practically whispering, "How do you know that?"

"Almost everyone here knew. They weren't secretive about it. Then, last week, Marissa's husband confronted her about it. Right here, right in front of me in the lobby."

"Oh my gosh! What did Marissa say?"

"She basically told him to get lost, said she couldn't care less what he thought, and that her lawyer would be in touch. Of course, she didn't say it all calmly like that. She was shouting, screeching like a banshee, but that was the gist of it."

"Wowzers."

"Yeah. From what I gathered, he'd just found out about the affair, and, man, was he hot."

"I don't blame him. I would be too. I don't know if I'd have it out with my spouse like that, but yeah, when you're mad, you're mad."

"And he was."

"Did you tell the police about this?" Jenny's sideways look was a clear indication that she hadn't said a word. "You really should," I encouraged her. "Trust me, it's an important detail."

People needed to start talking. I had no idea if Claire had taken my advice and shared her suspicions about Mr. Aldrich with the police, but I had a feeling she hadn't. Aside from that, the more theories Detective Blackwell had to investigate, the less inclined she would be to focus on me. Of course, I could tell the detective all this, but she'd be more prone to believe it if the story didn't come from me. I was kind of surprised that Jenny had kept mum about it. But I guess it's one thing to gossip about a murder and an entirely different thing to get involved with it, especially when it included your coworkers. "I understand you have some reservations, but just think about it," I said with an encouraging smile.

Jenny nodded. "The police did say to call them if we had any information."

"I'm sure you could make it anonymous."

Her eyes brightened at that. "Yeah, you're right. I could definitely do that."

With that settled, I moved on to the real reason for my visit. "So, I was wondering if you could help me. I was hoping to get some face time with Mr. Aldrich this morning."

Jenny looked at me like I had lost my mind. I knew it would be hard to get in with the CEO, but not impossible. "It's just… I don't… He has a very packed schedule," Jenny stammered.

"I know, but I only need five minutes. Is there any way you could squeeze me in somewhere, or maybe give me a heads-up about his schedule so I could "'bump into him'" for a chat? Even the elevator would work."

Jenny brought up what I assume to be Mr. Aldrich's schedule on her computer. I peered around her and saw blocks of color, indicating lunches and meetings, one stacked on top of the other. She was right; he was a very busy man. I could barely make out the writing, but it looked like he had a massage scheduled in thirty minutes. That would have to do. I told Jenny that maybe another day would work better and I would call his secretary directly to set something up. Jenny looked relieved that I had dropped the request. I told her it was nice to meet her and chat, reminded her to drop an anonymous tip for the police, and then walked out the front door and to my car.

I had a plan. A crazy plan, and I wasn't sure if I could

pull it off. If I got caught, it would most likely mean jail time, especially if Detective Blackwell was called. And orange jumpsuits were not my thing!

11

It was a good thing I had dressed in business attire that day—a black skirt with a floral silk blouse—or I would've never been able to pull off my big plan. Various news outlets seemed to take residence outside of the building, which only added to my cover. I spotted Cee Cee front and center, motioning to the building behind her while reporting an "update" to the curious minds. The news of Marissa's and Sterling's deaths had rocked the entertainment industry, and the national media outlets just picked up on the story, creating a heightened sense of mystery and speculation. The twenty-four-hour news coverage had to be brutal for the victims' families, not to mention the employees of DSC.

I sat in my car and gave myself a little pep talk. "Okay, when all this is over, you can enjoy a relaxing day of shopping therapy ... if you don't get thrown in the slammer, that is." When the next wave of employees arrived, I made my move. I followed the group of ladies to the side entrance and allowed them to swipe their key fobs, grabbing the door and holding it open for them. As the last one came through, I turned and tagged along behind her, blending in as if I knew exactly where I was headed, even though I had no idea where Mr. Aldrich's massage would take place. I figured it had to be some place close to his office, so that's where I headed. I had pretty much trespassed all over the entire first floor and hadn't recalled seeing the CEO's office, which meant it had to be upstairs. I found the conference room first, where the gala had taken place. Some round tables draped in white cloths were off to the side and a few pieces of confetti were scattered on the floor, the only remnants of the celebration. The next door I tried was locked. However, I struck gold with the third door, which was a good thing because I really didn't want to make small talk with the gentleman walking toward me.

I left the hallway and stepped into a spa room.

A massage table was set up in the middle of the private room, which was purple and had a small half-bath tucked away in the corner. On the counter, a variety of sheets and blankets had been set out next to the towel warmer. A bottle of oil sat warming in the heater as well. There was even an iPod playing soft, soothing music—a combination of instrumental mixed with rolling waves. Mixed scents of lavender and chamomile infused my nose and I almost sneezed again. Why couldn't I enjoy the beauty of nature just once?

Everything seemed to be set for the next client when a petite, dark-haired, perfectly tanned woman entered the room and saw me. "You're not Mr. Aldrich," she said in a wary voice."

I played it casual and acted like I worked there. "Oh, yeah, he cancelled his appointment. The front desk wanted me to let you know. I'm a temporary filling in for..." I searched my brain and thought of a common name for a perky girl who might work in a place like this. Thankfully, I didn't have to think long because the massage therapist filled in a name for me.

"—Amber?"

"Yes, that's right. Amber." *Whew!* Bullet dodged.

Relief washed over her at that statement. "Oh, okay." She seemed to want to be anywhere but there in that moment anyway, so I said, "If you want, you can leave everything set up here for your next appointment. Hey, I heard they are offering iced coffees for just ninety-nine cents in the café downstairs. You look like you could use a pick-me-up."

She didn't waste any time on her escape as she gathered her purse and phone. "You have no idea. It's been weird around here since the ... you know." Her eyes glanced sideways as if checking if anyone was listening. "Okay, nice meeting you. My next appointment's not until noon. See you around."

Phase one was complete.

I wasn't a licensed or trained massage therapist, but Finn never seemed to complain. Speaking of the guy, I checked my phone and saw that he had called. Finally. I had mixed emotions about catching up with him, but I had cooled down enough to at least hear him out. If he had something to say. If not, I'd just be arranging a time to pick up my stuff from the hotel and be on my way. I could FedEx his toothbrush from my apartment back to him another day, or maybe keep it and use it to clean my toilet.

I looked at my watch. Show time.

"Who are you?" Mr. Aldrich asked in the same brash British voice that I had come to expect. I always thought British accents sounded very sophisticated, but coming out of Mr. CEO's mouth, it was downright intimidating.

"I'm sorry, I'm Amber. I'll be doing your massage today. If you'd like, I'll step out so you can get ready. Your sheet's right here. Go ahead and get comfortable on the table and I'll knock before I come back in." I didn't give the man much of a chance to protest as I made my way out of the room. When I reentered, I was shocked to see that he had opted to forgo the sheet. However, and thankfully, he hadn't taken off all his clothing, now sporting a pair of cartoon-themed boxers. I guess the man had a sense of humor after all.

Mr. Aldrich wasn't very talkative, which I understood. I personally didn't like it when the massage therapist talked my ears off during my massages. I was there to relax, not have a pow-wow session with a girlfriend. However, I wasn't there rubbing warm oil on the old kook for fun. The man's shoulders were like two giant knots. The tension was unbelievable and I told him, "Your shoulders are really stiff. Let me know if I go too deep in that area." My comment was rewarded with a grunt. However, somewhere during the kneading and the rubbing, my magic fingers seemed to do the trick and Mr. Aldrich opened up to me as tension melted off his shoulders.

"I tell you what, these murders are bad for business." I started to sympathize, but before I could, he changed the direction of the conversation. "The ratings, though, are through the roof!" I could only imagine how important ratings were to a network's CEO, but even I was shocked at the bluntness of his statement. "You know, Marissa was a firecracker. She was never going to get the prime-time gig. She wasn't wholesome enough, and I told her that."

"Bet that went over really well."

"Let me tell you, she didn't like to hear it, but it was true. I thought she'd make a good executive, though, and I told her that too. We have a tough job, living and dying by the ratings. One bad season is all it takes for the board to consider replacing you. It's a lot of stress, a lot of pressure.

Takes a certain personality. Marissa had it. She didn't take that as a compliment; she wanted to be on camera. There was nothing I could do. She was just too harsh for camera work. Bottom line: You could see right through her pretty face."

Ouch.

"People would beg me for the type of opportunity I was willing to give her, but she didn't want it. She took it as an insult."

I had moved on to massaging Mr. Aldrich's forearms and hands. It seemed the more he loosened up, the more he was willing to say.

"So, what happened?" I asked.

"She went nuts, that's what! Took out her anger by snapping my putter in half. I thought she was going to chuck the club at my head." Mr. Aldrich gave an amused chuckle and I could tell that he really did find it quite humorous. "I know it sounds wrong, but I appreciated her enthusiasm."

I thought to myself that if Detective Blackwell had heard half of this story, she would request a private audience with the CEO. Of course, he would never let that happen without his lawyers present, and I highly doubted he was about to willingly give up any information. The CEO must've sensed my thoughts when he said, "Don't go thinking I had anything to do with that poor girl's demise. I thought she was talented. In any light, it doesn't matter, even if the police did find out about our little confrontation. My alibi's as tight as The Queen's purse, with business meetings all afternoon and the gala in the evening. Several people can attest to that. I didn't have a moment's peace."

"I highly doubt anyone would suspect you." Okay, so I was totally brown-nosing here, but maybe I'd get a good tip. My hands were aching. Surely the hour had to be about up?

"It's a shame she was murdered though. She would've made one heck of an executive. Now we just need to get this mess quickly cleaned up for the network's rating tank. It's always about the ratings."

"And Sterling?" I asked. "Wasn't that his name?" I moved down to the man's legs and wasn't even sure what muscles I was kneading, but I just kept working.

"Sterling thought with his Johnson, and I bet that's why he's dead. You can mark my words on that. I tried to warn him, but the man never listened."

Someone knocked on the door and my heart jumped into my throat. I thought about ignoring it, but the person knocked again, louder this time. "Excuse me." I wiped my hands on a towel and partially slid across the floor to the door (apparently, I had been a little overzealous with the oil), and opened it a crack, peering out. The light seemed so bright compared to the dim room I was in.

"Yes?" I said, blinking a few times to help my eyes adjust. I found myself answering a professional-looking woman in a black pencil skirt and white shirt. She was all-business with her dark hair pulled back into a perfect bun.

"Who are you?" The woman asked.

"I'm—" Shoot, what name had I given Mr. Aldrich?

"Mrs. Peters, what do you need?" Mr. Aldrich barked from the table. I stepped partially behind the door to give him a clear line to the woman.

"Sorry, sir, but there's a detective here to see you."

Eep! I kept that interjection to myself, or at least I hoped I did.

Mr. Aldrich grunted. I would've liked to take that as a compliment to my massage technique, but it was probably more that he really didn't want to talk with the woman. Me?

I was trying to not pee my pants as I thought of how I would escape.

"If you would, give us a few minutes to just wrap up here and then maybe have the detective meet Mr. Aldrich in his office?" I said the last part to Mr. Aldrich to see what he thought of it.

"Yes, do that."

"Will do," the woman replied.

I nodded my head at the woman and shut the door behind her, trying not to panic. I couldn't hide out in the massage room all morning—the *real* therapist would be back soon—but I didn't want Detective Blackwell to see me either.

"Well sir, I guess that about wraps it up for us today," I said, walking back toward the table and grabbing a towel to wipe my hands off some more.

Mr. Aldrich slowly sat up and looked at me expectantly. I was a little slow on the uptake, wondering what in the world he was waiting for.

"Well, aren't you going to leave so I can get dressed?" he said after a minute.

"Yes, of course. Oh my goodness, sorry." In my panic, I had totally forgotten spa etiquette. I guess I had been hoping he would just go to the bathroom and get dressed, so I could've hidden out in the room until I knew he was in a meeting with the detective.

I looked around for my purse. "Let me just grab something and I'll be right out of your way." I walked behind the table and grabbed my purse off the counter. There was no way I was hanging out in the hallway or coming back in to reset the room.

I mumbled something lame about hoping he had enjoyed the massage, said a quick prayer, and opened the door. Detective Blackwell was standing right at the end of the hallway in front of the elevators. Mrs. Peters was talking to her while the detective looked around, examining every detail.

"Sugar," I said under my breath. I turned and headed in the opposite direction, reminding myself not to run. Soon I could disappear around the corner and maybe hide out in a bathroom or something for a while. I rounded the corner and thankfully spotted a stairwell up ahead. Without looking back, I swung the door open and smacked it right into Skip the Producer's face.

"Oh my goodness, I'm so sorry."

Skip the Producer took a step back and covered his face. "Am I bleeding?" he asked, although I couldn't tell because his hand was covering his nose.

"Let me see." He lowered his hand and everything looked okay, well that is, if his nose had always curved a little to the right.

"I'm so sorry, I wasn't watching where I was going. Again."

"I thought you said you weren't coming back?" He rubbed his nose.

"Change in plans, but I'm taking off now. I swear."

He looked at me like he didn't believe me for a second. He was probably right.

12

My heart hammered in my chest, even when I was safely back in my truck. My phone rang and I slapped my hand over my chest. "Sweet sugar!" It was my mom. I sent that call right to voicemail. Sorry, Mom. I needed to calm myself before I talked to her. However, holding my phone reminded me that Finn had called. Did I want to talk to him? I supposed there was no time like the present to get this over with.

I took a deep breath and chickened out, sending Finn a text instead. A simple one that said: "*Hey, where are you?*"

The little bubble below his text message indicated he was replying, but then nothing. I waited, thinking maybe he had to reorganize his thoughts, but two minutes went by and still nothing. The only thing that came across my screen was the time stamp that showed he had read my message. I sat back and thought about what that meant. It was clear to me that he had changed his mind and he didn't want to talk to me, or he couldn't at that moment, for whatever reason. It was ridiculous and I didn't have time to deal with it.

I moved on to my next order of business.

I thought back to the case. I wasn't sure what to make of Mr. Aldrich. He seemed to appreciate the characteristics in people that others tried to discourage: ruthlessness, aggression, a thirst for success. I got the feeling he'd respected Marissa. Obviously, he wouldn't have offered to mentor her if not. Sterling? Not so much. Mr. Aldrich said it was always all about the ratings and Sterling constantly delivered. I would bet any money that's why he was going to still be part of the network and Tess was on her way out. If anything, the CEO's warning to Sterling was a reminder not to screw up the status quo.

Having vetted Mr. Aldrich, I next wanted to speak with Marissa's husband. I tried to see the case from his perspective. What were his motives? First, his wife was having an affair, a high-profile one, and she didn't even try to be inconspicuous. I wondered why. What had been her end-game? And then I thought again about how Marissa had been murdered. Dr. Stewart, being a surgeon, would surely know where to stab a person for maximum impact. Like I said, I did think this was a crime of passion, a split-second decision, considering how she was murdered. No one in their right mind would've murdered someone on-set. For all the murderer knew, there were security cameras or a private camera hidden somewhere. This murder hadn't been thought through. Toss in Dr. Stewart's argument with his wife the day before, and he definitely had enough anger to commit the crime. One question remained: Had he been at the gala?

Sterling's murder, on the other hand? That one I wasn't so sure about. It wouldn't be the first time a husband killed his wife and her lover. So, that theory wasn't totally out of left field, but I didn't know enough about Sterling's death to make that claim. I wished I knew how he died. The cause of death would've added credibility to the whole suicide angle, or maybe steer the police toward Dr. Stewart. What I needed now was a private audience with the MD. How was I going to work that out?

I was done pretending to be a massage therapist. That had worked once, but I wasn't taking any chances. A new strategy was in order. I could've crashed the funeral, but I did have some respect for the dead, so that was below my standards. I could've stopped by their house with a covered dish, but that seemed too cliché. I reminded myself of the KISS method (Keep It Simple, Stupid). I called the office to make an appointment, even though I had no idea how long it would take to get in. Most plastic surgeons, especially the ones in high demand, often had extensive waiting lists. But it was a place to start.

When I called the office, I explained to the receptionist my dilemma, sort of. "Hi, my name's Ziva Diaz. I actually live out of town, but my friend gave me Dr. Stewart's name and told me he was the best in the business. Anyway, I'm only in town for a couple of days and I would love to get in for a consultation with him if that's possible?"

I was waiting for her to say no, but she was quite accommodating. "You know, I did have a cancellation for tomorrow morning at 10 A.M. Would something like that work for you?"

"Absolutely. I'll take it."

"Okay, and what would you like to see the doctor for?"

"Um..." What did I want to see him for? Ugh... I may not have a smoking-hot body, but I'd never really considered going under the knife before.

"It's okay, honey, this is a judgement-free zone."

"It's not that, sorry, I was just distracted for a minute. I'd like to see him for a breast augmentation." The words slipped out of my mouth before I could stop them. Truth? My boobs were a little pathetic. I thought I had gotten over it. Apparently, I hadn't. It was probably the most believable cover anyway, so I ran with it. Besides, I would've sounded like a total nut case if I switched it to something else.

"Wonderful. Well, Dr. Stewart is the best. I'm so happy that we're able to fit you in. If you could just provide me with your email address, I'll go ahead and send you a link for a little pre-appointment questionnaire and get you registered for tomorrow."

I stared at my phone and a bubble formed in my stomach. *What the heck did I just get myself into?*

~

My morning had been quite productive and I deserved a little bit of *me time*, but I knew I wouldn't be able to relax until I connected with Finn. I drove past the hotel where we'd stayed, but he would've been checked out by now, so I wasn't surprised this time to see his truck was no longer parked there. If I didn't track him down, I'd have to stop back there and see if he had left my belongings behind. That would've been cold, but not as shocking as it would've been a couple of days ago.

I checked my phone and he still hadn't called or texted back.

I called once, spinning a silver band on my finger with every unanswered ring, until his voicemail came on and I hung up. And then I did what any psychotic person would do. I called back. Again, and again, and again. When that didn't work, I tried texting. Not once or twice, but half a dozen messages ranging from "*Hello?*" to "*What the heck, yo?*" Still no response. Well, until Finn turned off his phone.

"Oh no he didn't!" I gave my phone attitude when I tried calling Finn again and it went straight to voicemail—a clear indication it had been powered off. I knew Finn had seen my calls and purposely ignored them, which made me go from zero to psycho in a flash. It was one of my pet peeves and he knew that. I was seeing red, ready to hunt him down. This man was about to experience the full wrath of my mad investigating skills.

I tried to think back if he had given me any details about the person he was meeting and where they'd planned to meet. I had to admit I hadn't paid much attention—a bit too preoccupied with my national television debut. For all I knew, he could've told me the name of the marina his buddy worked at, but I couldn't recall. It was time I took off my girlfriend hat and put on my detective one to look at the clues. Think, Ziva, think. I recalled bits and pieces of our conversation on the car ride down here. Finn was excited, I realized that now. I thought, at first, he was just feeding off my jitters, but it turned out he had a big deal in the works. *The guy's name is Kevin.* I remembered Finn telling me stories about this guy on Instagram who moved down to Tampa and was killing it with charter business. But that was all I got.

Meditation. That's what I needed. If I was going to try to recall information from a week before, I needed to get into the right state of mind. One would think that the beach would be a relaxing place to try to sit and meditate, but I had grown leery of the golden sands. At least for now. What had Izzy said about the crystal she'd given me? That it would raise my vibrations with positive energy and offer some clarity? I retrieved the stone out of my purse and placed it in the palm of my hand. It was ridiculous to think that this little piece of rock could do anything other than look pretty, but I decided to pour some energy into it and see if it would help me clear my mind. If not, maybe I could just call Izzy and see if her clairvoyant skills picked up any clues.

I held the stone in my hand and, this time, I felt absolutely nothing. After sitting in my truck for five minutes playing with the rock, I still had no answers. Instead of feeling calm or renewed, I was frustrated. Blocked, as Izzy would put it.

I decided to do things more my way and simply reached out to my nana to give me a hand. My nana was the best guardian angel I could ever ask for. She found little ways to always let me know she was there, like the ever-present ladybug that always seemed to land on my shoulder, the smell of her rose perfume on a Sunday morning, or every time I looked at the clock and saw that the minute hand was at twenty-seven. Always twenty-seven, the age I was when she left me, but she would always remain in my heart. I thought love was a much more powerful connection than a crystal, and I used that love to talk to my grandma every day.

So, that's exactly what I did. I talked to my grandma and asked her what I could do. I probably should have done more listening than talking, but I let it all spill out. I found myself asking my grandma not only what I should do and where Finn was, but also if he was even worth my time of trying to track him down. All I got in return was an overwhelming feeling of love, and I had trouble determining if she was saying how much she loved me or if she was referring to how much I had loved Finn. Notice I said *had* because, at that moment, I wasn't feeling very amorous. Murderous was more like it. Where was a medium when you needed one?

I pulled out of the parking lot and decided to do this old-school style, driving by the various marinas to see if I spotted him.

An hour later, I was beyond frustrated. I needed to start coming up with a better plan. Do you know how many marinas there are in the Tampa Bay area? It's a bit ridiculous. I wasn't going to give up though. I looked over at my phone and had an epiphany. Finn's phone might have been turned off, but I'd guarantee he still had it on him. We recently had signed up to share a plan with our wireless provider (see, I told you I was better in the commitment department!) and as a result, our phones were synched. I couldn't believe I hadn't thought of it sooner. All I had to do was log in to the "Find My Phone" app and BAM! There he was. "Gotcha." Finn's flashing blue orb was awfully close to mine. I zoomed and read "Bayshore Marina." He was not more than a mile away.

I spotted his truck before I saw him. I always did like his truck. It was such a man ride with its super-sized wheels, all-leather interior, and kicking sound system. I flipped down the sun visor of my pickup and checked my makeup in the mirror. Oh no, this would not do. I took a second to freshen up my lipstick and popped a chocolate kiss in my mouth for added measure. The chocolate melted and sent liquid courage to my tummy, giving the butterflies something to snack on.

"Okay, let's do this."

I was halfway down the front boardwalk when I saw him, bare chested, straddling a cooler, and it wouldn't be right if he didn't have a can of Coke in his hand. Hey, I didn't mind as long as he drank it shirtless. This was one vice of his I could live with. But then I remembered, he was the one who *couldn't live with me*, for whatever reason, and I wanted to cry. I swallowed my insecurities and thought maybe I had it all wrong, maybe we just needed to talk. (I've been told that I'm prone to over-reacting.) I thought maybe that was it, and I was suddenly excited to see Finn. That is, until I saw them—the girls, wearing skimpy bikinis with their long lush locks blowing in the wind.

One by one the girls paraded up from down below the boat's galley, like beauty pageant contestants in a swimsuit competition. My stomach dropped. Finn stood up as if he had been waiting for them, four of them in total, as they crowded around him and another guy, who I assumed was the infamous Kevin. He was shirtless as well, but I no longer found either one of the men attractive.

A man wearing salmon-colored shorts and a white button down stepped on the boat and began positioning the women. He had an impressive-looking camera strapped across his shoulder and started snapping away. It took my mind a minute to catch up. This was obviously a photoshoot of some sort, but I didn't care what it was for. I didn't like the fact that there were girls all over the guy I still considered mine, even if his feelings weren't the same for me.

I turned and hightailed it off the docks, not wanting him to see me in that state, tears in my eyes and anger bubbling up in my throat. I stifled my emotions and found it much easier to just be angry. Here I had been trying to get ahold of him and give him the benefit of the doubt, while he had turned off his phone so he could prance around shirtless with a bunch of supermodels. What a jerk. I glanced behind my shoulder and shot him the evil eye. He never saw me, but at that moment, he lost his footing and hit the deck. I smirked and cast my eyes upward. "Thanks, Nana. I owe you one."

13

Izzy called me right when I was in the middle of some nasty gridlock traffic and in the throes of road rage. There's nothing worse than wanting to floor the gas pedal only to end up stuck, puttering along at less than five miles per hour.

"What?" I snapped into the phone before I could collect myself. "Sorry, girl, I meant to say hello."

"Aha, I see Mercury's still not doing you any favors with your communication skills." I let my manager have that one.

"You have no idea, or maybe you do, being you and all that, but I don't want to go there right now. What do you have for me?"

"Definitely something to cheer you up. I just got off the phone with the Lavish spa manager and they loved the samples we sent them. And… They want you to come to New York next week."

This was big. Bigger than big. Huge. Lavish did billions of dollars in sales every single year. Billions. I couldn't fathom what this could do for my company, let alone my pocketbook. "You told him yes, right?!" Make that absolutely freaking yes.

"Your flight leaves Friday at 6:55 A.M." I didn't even care that she had booked me on a flight at the crack of dawn.

"Sweet." I bubbled over inside, and it came through in my voice.

"And that's not all. You know Poppy Harlow?"

I was pretty sure everyone knew Poppy Harlow. She was an A-list starlet of the moment, packing the seats for the summer blockbuster and walking the red carpet at every event.

"Her rep called, and she loves it."

I had written off Izzy's suggestion to send out free samples to all the celebrity representatives she could track down, thinking our marketing dollars could be better invested elsewhere, but Izzy had been right, or it looked as if she would be. I was speechless, as in holding-the-phone, staring-at-the-screen speechless. It was probably a good thing that I was stuck in traffic at that moment, because I couldn't even focus to speak, let alone drive.

"You there, love?"

"Yeah, sorry just, oh my goodness."

"The best is yet to come. What did I tell you? I told you your little shop here was just the beginning."

She had. The day I hired Izzy, she walked into my store and shared a vision with me that I hadn't even been able to admit to myself. Her passion and enthusiasm for Sugar & Sass was almost as great as mine.

"Listen, I'm going to forward the email exchange between the Lavish's manager and me for you to check out. If you want to talk strategy for your meeting next week, or if you need me to do anything else, let me know."

"Yeah, I'll read it right away, and I definitely want to talk strategy with you. Just give me a little bit, I'm in my car right now, and I'll call you back later."

"Sounds lovely. You know where to find me."

With that she clicked off and my day seemed so much brighter. My love life may have been in the toilet, but my business was soaring.

~

I DIDN'T GO STRAIGHT BACK to the hotel but instead pulled over in a mall parking lot. My emotions were flying off into all different directions and, honestly, I wasn't sure which way I wanted to run.

So, I threw myself into my work. I had been toying with the idea of adding a perfume line to my product offering, and there was nothing like a little holistic homework to help settle my thoughts. I used my phone to locate a nearby wellness store and pointed my car in that direction.

When I walked into the store, I was instantly struck by the electric charge all around. I swear, even the hair on my arms was standing up and I was as energized as if I had slammed a venti chai latte. Talk about a caffeine rush. The front of the store had several round tables draped in white tablecloths, with little glass bowls set about, full of rocks and crystals. I had no idea so many specialty stones existed. I walked around looking at the ones that caught my fancy—the pink ones, of course—and read their descriptions. Some promised mental clarity, increased wealth, or other calming properties.

I skipped reading the rest of the descriptions as I was suddenly drawn to the beaded jewelry on the wall. For an instant, I forgot why I came to the store in the first place. The chipped crystal bracelets were gorgeous. I fingered the rose quartz one and, at only five dollars, I knew I would be taking it home with me. In fact, a couple others called my name and I knew they would make a gorgeous collage on my wrist. I finally looked over at the essential oils display and remembered my mission.

An hour later, I had shopping bags full of more oils than I would've ever needed, and a determination to create something awesome. The wellness store turned out to be just what I needed, even though it wasn't quite the retail therapy I'd had in mind. Irene, the shop's owner, was a lovely woman who knew more about oils and holistic healing than I thought possible. She and Izzy could've been BFFs.

"Your aura—" she started with.

"—is all murky. I know. I'm working on it."

"I have a crystal that can help with that."

I reached into my pocket and pulled out the smooth, pink stone. Irene stopped mid-track. "One of my good friends is sort of my spiritual guru."

"She's a good friend to have then."

"That she is."

"Good luck. I'd love to see what you come up with."

"Thanks so much. I'll have to stop in again."

I left the wellness store revived and ready to get to work.

I DUMPED my goodies out on the feather-down duvet and pulled the coffee table over, setting up a work station. Irene also stocked roller bottles, so I was literally ready to roll.

When it comes to designing perfume, it seems simple at first—mix your carrier oil, some alcohol, a splash of water, and your scents—until you consider all the variations. There are half a dozen carrier oils at least, and essential oils?

Irene had at least eighty. I decided to try almond oil as my carrier. I had previously been toying with a romantic blend of rose, pink grapefruit, and vetiver, but my heart just wasn't into it. Besides, the rose oil kept making me sneeze. Instead, I decided to go with two different scents: one that was bright and fresh with grapefruit, juniper, and ginger; and another that was sweet and sensuous with sweet orange, sandalwood, and ylang ylang. I also picked up some lavender, chamomile, and vanilla because I needed a little relaxation blend right about then.

Much like an artist blends pigments to create the perfect shade of paint, I planned to blend scents to create a signature fragrance. And just like an artist applies paint in layers, that is also how perfume is created, with each layer represented by a note—top note, middle note, and base note. The notes represented the order in which they are recognized by the human senses. Top notes are the lightest of all, and the one recognized immediately when applying the fragrance. As the top notes fade, the middle notes make their appearance, lasting the longest in creating the heart of the fragrance, which is what they're sometimes called. And finally, the base notes take over, creating the lasting impression that lingers all day.

Right now, my base note was all wrong. All I was getting was a heavy dose of juniper, which was not very appealing. My life stunk in all sorts of ways at that moment.

14

A knock on the door snapped me out of my moment of Zen. If Finn had somehow tracked me down, I wasn't sure I wanted to speak with him; at least, not in that moment. I looked out the peep hole of my hotel door and saw Detective Blackwell's eagle eye staring back at me.

"Ms. Diaz?"

I didn't have to answer the door and I knew I was within my rights to not speak to the woman, but I had a feeling that would only make matters worse and cause me to look guilty. I had nothing to hide and the quicker I talked to the woman, the sooner I could get back to work.

I swung the door open. "Detective, how lovely to see you," I said, the sarcasm thick in my voice. The detective entered my room, even though she hadn't been invited, and surveyed the supplies. I could only imagine what all the little vials must have looked like to her, but she didn't comment.

"Do I need a lawyer?" I straight up asked the woman. I was starting to feel like I should've gotten one the first go around.

Detective Blackwell shrugged her shoulders. "I don't know, do you?"

Touché.

I then thought of something the detective might want to know, and might have her backing off me a bit. "Not sure if you heard, but Sterling and Marissa were having an affair."

The detective's eyebrows shot up, but she tried to play it casual. "I'm sorry, but I don't buy that tabloid trash," she shot back, dismissing my tip.

"Um, I'm pretty sure it's common knowledge. Just ask anyone at DSC. I just thought you might want to look into it."

"Are you trying to tell me how to do my job?"

Oh brother.

I turned my back to the detective and walked over to the fridge to retrieve a bottle of water. The detective took it as an opening to begin her questioning. "Have you ever had any cosmetic procedures done?"

The question stopped me mid-water bottle to my mouth. I wondered if the detective knew that I made a doctor's appointment for the next morning. *But, how could she, unless she bugged my phone?! Or, maybe she had a mole removed at Dr. Stewart's office?* "I have no idea where you're going with this, but no, I haven't. If you know much about me and my company, you would know that I prefer more natural beauty remedies."

"Not even Botox?"

"Botox? Yeah, no." I left it at that. Truth be told, I knew I had my nana's good genes to thank for my smooth face and even skin tone, rather than any cream or lotion.

"It would be fitting for a beauty consultant to plump up her face, make her products appear more effective, don't you think?"

If looks could kill, the detective would've dropped dead right there as I shot daggers at her. She picked up right away that she'd offered me the worst insult possible.

"Heard you left town. Something got you a little ... on edge?"

"Work emergency back home. You know I'm not from here, right?"

"But you rented a car."

"Because Finn had business here." Detective Blackwell stared at me, as if looking for any cracks in my complexion, or my story.

"Is there anything else?" I asked, sending her subliminal messages to leave. She didn't seem to get them.

"Nice hotel room you have here."

I looked around the room. "Yeah, I like it." I wasn't sure that my senses were renewed as the hotel had promised, but if I ever finished this fragrance, maybe they would be.

"Why the change?"

"Better room service." Or so I had heard.

"You're staying alone." It wasn't a question.

"Excuse me?"

"Did your boyfriend break up with you, or has he suddenly gone *missing*?" Detective Blackwell used air quotes around the last word. "Should we send out a search party or just bring you in for questioning?"

"What?"

"Got a little taste of blood and now you just can't stop, or is it another woman? Yeah, I can see that right from the look on your face. He's tossed you out and has already hooked up with someone else. Is she a blonde?" The detective had slowly encroached on my personal space until she was inches from my face. Her flaky black eyeliner and clumpy eyelashes stared at me, daring me to fight back.

Her plan had almost worked. The woman had my blood boiling and I was about to let her have it, but then I took a step back and laughed. I seriously laughed in the woman's face.

"Oh my gosh, that's it. You've got nothing on me, so you're trying to set me off. See if you can trip me up. You know what? I feel sorry for Marissa's and Sterling's families. They deserve a better detective on this case."

It was Detective Blackwell's turn to get angry. "You little brat."

"Well, that's professional of you."

"I'll have you know—"

"—No, I'll have you know that we're through. It's time for you to leave, and next time you feel like stopping by ... don't. You can call my lawyer." I walked over to the door and held it open, giving her a little smile as she stormed out. I was one hundred percent done being nice.

IT HAD TAKEN me longer than I wanted to admit to calm down after Detective Blackwell's little visit. I had to remind myself more than once that she was the inept one and was clueless when it came to my relationship with Finn, but damn her, she put the idea in my head that Finn was seeing someone else and I couldn't let it go. I inhaled enough lavender after she left that I should've been comatose, but I was still a little edgy while getting ready to meet Cee Cee. Hopefully that tête-à-tête would be more productive.

With my stomach in knots, I took a bit more time than usual to get ready, or maybe I wanted to prove to myself that I still had *it*, you know, sex appeal. I put spiral curls in my long chocolate locks, busted out my gold eyeliner and bronze eyeshadows, and finished off the look with the nude lipstick. I smacked my lips together and took a step back to look in the mirror, turning my head from side to side. Oh yeah, I still had it.

Dockside was a small seaside waterfront bar not too far from my hotel. I could've easily walked the distance to the canals, but not with the heels I had chosen to wear. I had planned on wearing this romper and cork heel outfit for Finn, but yeah, whatever.

Cee Cee pulled in the parking lot right after me and we parked next to one another. Although she didn't know me yet, I recognized her right away and greeted her when she opened the door.

"Cee Cee? Hi, I'm Ziva Diaz."

"Thanks so much for reaching out. I think we'll have lots to talk about."

"That's what I'm hoping anyway." We took a table out back on the deck in the front corner, overlooking the calm waters. The restaurant wasn't a dive bar, but it wasn't anything fancy either. It definitely wasn't the type of place I'd expect to find Cee Cee Williams, and that's what made it the perfect location to meet up.

We took a few moments for small chat while waiting for drinks to arrive, to get a feel for one another. Cee Cee was from out west, a California girl who didn't care where she was as long as the ocean was nearby. I could one hundred percent relate to that. Well, maybe ninety percent. If I kept finding dead bodies by the ocean, I planned to move to the desert.

We switched to talking about the case when our cocktails were set in front of us.

"So, the Marissa affair," Cee Cee began.

"Is that what they're calling it now?"

"It's catchy. So, you were telling me that you had some information."

"Here's what I know, just from snooping around and finding the bodies. One, Marissa didn't put up a fight. Two, a lot of people couldn't stand her."

Her eyes went wide. "Tell me more."

I filled Cee Cee in on what I had learned from Claire, Tess, and Mr. Aldrich and how Marissa looked when I found her. I skipped over the private conversation between Mr. Aldrich and Sterling. I didn't need that to be breaking news on *Entertainment Now*.

"So, you see, it seems like everyone who had a motive to kill her was at the gala Friday night. Well, everyone except for her husband."

"Oh no, he was there."

"What? He was?"

"Not as a guest, but witnesses placed him in the parking lot that evening."

"Shut up!" Could there possibly have been any more evidence stacked against the guy? Why Detective Blackwell was still wasting her time with me was completely beyond me.

"And Marissa's time of death?" I was hoping that Cee Cee had an answer to that question.

"Around 6:45 P.M. That's what my sources tell me."

"So, right as the gala was kicking off." Any one of the guests could have killed her. It was like a game of Clue, and I wasn't sure how I felt about that.

"It's her husband though, I'm telling you."

"You sound confident." I had my reasons for suspecting him, but I was curious to hear hers.

"His wife's leaving him. He's embarrassed. He's going to be out a ton of money, which angers him. Then he sees his wife all glammed up, walking the red carpet? SNAP. He goes ballistic and kills her."

I could easily see the picture Cee Cee had painted.

"I'm meeting him tomorrow."

"You're what?" She almost choked on her drink.

"I have an appointment with Dr. Stewart in the morning. I'll let you know what I find out."

"You're crazy, and I'm totally jealous I didn't think to do that. Of course, I wouldn't have been able to pull it off, but I would have had fun trying."

"I'll keep you posted." I smiled and sipped my drink.

She returned the smirk. "Yes, please do."

15

The next morning, my knees were bouncing so hard it made the keys in the ignition jingle. My emotions were all over the place. I reminded myself that this was an interview, whether the doctor realized it or not. The plastic surgery appointment was just my cover. If I thought of it like that and nothing more, then it was a role I would be able to play.

When I walked in the office, I heard a needle scratching across a spinning record inside my head. *Hold up. Rewind. What is this place?* I had to stop myself from stepping back outside and rereading the sign to make sure I was at the right spot. Talk about a Zen-like atmosphere. I wasn't sure if I was there to get a massage or talk about breast augmentation. Maybe they offered both?

From the slate-tiled floors and white high-pile rugs, to the gray suede backless couches and the white potted cymbidium orchid on the accent table, the place screamed high-end. Even the receptionist desk, with its dark wood frame and pearl inlay, was impressive. I wanted to hate the place, but it appealed to my love of aesthetics and I found myself taking mental design notes. I liked to think that I worked with people's natural beauty. Dr. Stewart took that to a whole new level, but maybe there was room for both of us in this business. After all, I was all about making women love the way they look. I had a feeling Dr. Stewart was too.

After accepting a cool glass of lemon water, I was whisked back to a comfortable office space. The first part of my appointment was a short meeting with Dr. Stewart's assistant, Katie. She gave me a rundown of how the appointment would go, and I found myself second guessing my cover when it came to the agenda.

"Don't be nervous. Dr. S. is awesome. You're going to love him," she said, handing me a thick cotton robe to put on. "It opens in the front."

I offered her a weak smile and accepted the robe. *I should've just asked the man to meet me for coffee. That's what a sane person would do,* I thought while taking my top off. I blamed all of this on Finn. If he hadn't turned my world upside down, I would have been thinking more clearly. I was just about to get up and walk out when a decent-looking, silver-haired man wearing black scrubs and a megawatt smile walked in.

"Hi, Ziva. I'm Dr. Stewart. How are you?" He had a sense of calm about him that instantly made me relax. I accepted his warm handshake and found myself smiling in return. His assistant, Katie, rejoined us as well.

"So, Katie here tells me that you're interested in a breast augmentation." I nodded my head as if that were the truth. I mean, I guess it could be. You could definitely say that my Puerto Rican genes had only impacted one asset and that was of the bootylicious variety.

"How long have you been thinking about this?" *Um, since yesterday?* Okay, that wasn't what I said. "For quite a while.

I'm not sure exactly, but I have never been gifted up-top, if you know what I mean."

The doctor went on to talk to me about what my goals and expectations were, providing implant options and pros and cons of each along the way. Katie handed me a silicon implant to check out and I blushed when I realized I'd had a bit too much fun playing with the sucker. It was like a soft, squishy stress ball, or one of those water weenies I used to play with when I was a kid.

I was having a good time until the doctor said, "Okay, let's have a look." The next thing I knew, I was getting a breast exam, complete with a measuring tape and comments about my breast fold. *What is a breast fold?*

Katie then led me into another room to have some digital images taken. Striking a pose topless was not how I planned on this appointment going. I needed to find a way to take charge if I was going to ask any questions.

Ten minutes later, I was back in the consultation room, waiting for the doctor to rejoin us, and formulating my plan for questioning, when Dr. Stewart walked in with another implant in hand. Within a few seconds, the doctor had brought up my images on an impressive flat-screen computer monitor. Looking at my pictures, I concluded I was a little more flat-chested than I'd realized. Or maybe the enhanced images next to it gave that impression. Either way, it was a sight to behold.

Without warning, a woman flung the door open and barged right into the room. I couldn't have been more surprised if she'd kicked the door in. I jumped out of the chair, my eyes darting around for a place to hide, forgetting the fact that my breasts were practically on a Jumbotron for all to see. That was beside the point. This woman had crazy in her eyes.

"You!" She thrusted her finger out at Dr. Stewart. I was slightly relieved to see her take out her anger on him, and even more so when I realized she didn't have a weapon. "I trusted you, and you did this. You took Sterling away from me."

"Mary Jane, calm down. I know you're angry, I know you're hurt, so am I. I lost my wife too."

"You murdered her! Both of them! Don't try to act innocent. You will pay for this. I promise on my husband's grave, I will make you pay." The woman stormed out just as abruptly as she had entered the room, leaving Dr. Stewart completely deflated and me slightly bewildered. I replayed the conversation in my head and realized that the woman, Mary Jane, was Sterling's wife. Honestly, if it hadn't been for all the screaming and yelling, I would've said that the woman was beautiful. She definitely had a fiery spirit. Mary Jane looked much younger than I would've expected to be married to a guy like Sterling. The man was, after all, in his sixties and I thought he had been married for thirty years.

Dr. Stewart started to apologize once he found his manners, but I couldn't continue the charade. I quickly retrieved my purse off the hook and was planning on leaving when instead I blurted out, "I have a confession. I wasn't really here about a breast augmentation. In fact, I'm the one who found your wife's body and, honestly, I wanted to ask you a couple of questions."

"You what?" Dr. Stewart replied, but I knew he was following along, so I kept talking.

"I was hoping for a chance to talk with you to see if you could point me in the right direction. The detective on the case has been breathing down my neck, and she's a complete idiot."

Dr. Stewart just stared at me. I thought for a minute that

he was going to kick me out. I could tell the man didn't like the fact that I had lied to him, but he was smart and quickly realized that I could be an ally.

"I'm sorry, this is all just a bit much. You say that you found Marissa's body?" he said.

"I did. I was her last guest on Friday's show. I went back on-set to retrieve my cell phone when I came across her."

Dr. Stewart slowly nodded his head once to confirm that he understood.

"And the detective has you pegged for the murder?"

"Honestly, I don't know what the detective's problem is. Yes, I did find your wife's body; and yes, my interview with her on Friday didn't go so well; but that's the extent to which I knew her. Well, that and I also found Sterling's body on the beach." This time, the doctor cocked his head as if to say, "*You what*?" I took a deep breath and channeled my courage to continue, "I know, trust me. I really could've done without finding another dead body."

"Don't feel bad. They're not just looking at you. Here, why don't you follow me into my office and we can continue this conversation." I followed the doctor down the hall while he assured his staff that everything was all right. Apparently, Mary Jane had said some choice words to the receptionist, and the patients as well. It seemed a bit of damage control was in order. No one liked the thought of a murderer operating on them.

I checked out his office while he settled the staff. Just like him, his office was warm and inviting. He had medical degrees and certifications framed, along with pictures of him and Marissa and two adorable corgi pups. In fact, the small-framed print on his desk was of the two of them on a beach somewhere—Marissa smiling radiantly into the camera, wearing a red bikini and floppy straw hat. A gorgeous diamond pendant hung between her breasts, glinting in the sun. Dr. Stewart smiled down at her, totally in love. My heart broke for the man. I continued to scan the room. The walls had been painted the softest gray-blue, almost the same color as the doctor's eyes, which looked full of despair when I looked up at him as he entered the room. The confident man with the megawatt smile seemed to deflate. "It doesn't matter," he said, motioning toward the outside of his office. "Everyone is going to find out soon enough. Like I said, the police have already been to my house. I even let them search it, which my lawyer is furious about. I knew I shouldn't have let them, but I was just numb. Still am. I just wasn't expecting all of this. I know what's coming. The media, they've already started." I knew what the doctor was referring to. The story had quickly gained steam, making the jump from tabloid to prime-time. "They're already starting to speculate that it was me, bringing other experts in to discuss my motives, means, mental status. The detective already laid it out for me."

"I'm sure she did."

"But she's right. The divorce would've been pricey. She was murdered and then her boyfriend was murdered. To top it off, we had a fight right in the middle of the lobby at DSC the day before."

"Tell me you at least have a good alibi." I knew Cee Cee said he was spotted in the parking lot, but I didn't want to believe it.

"Sitting at home reading about anaplastic large-cell lymphoma? Not hardly."

I winced. I could admit that I could see where they would be coming from. As selfish as it sounds, I was partially relieved to see him take some of the pressure off me. That didn't let me off the hook, though, not when I saw how crushed he was.

"Marissa had just told me about the affair. I knew we had problems, but I didn't think they were that bad. Stupid of me to blow up with her at work, but I just had to talk to her and she wasn't returning my calls. She knew I didn't want to give her a divorce. Said I was being selfish. She was the one being selfish."

"How do you mean, exactly?"

The doctor stood up and paced the room, running his fingers through his hair. "She had grand visions of her and Sterling running the daytime network, being an inseparable and unstoppable *power couple*. Personally, I liked it better when she was the traffic reporter for TV 10." I must've raised my eyebrows because Dr. Stewart explained, "Not like that. I was happy for her success, but I liked it more before it went to her head. And her parents? They've always hated me. I was never good enough for their princess. I'm a frickin' plastic surgeon! But no, they've already accused me and, with their money, they'll make sure everyone believes I'm at fault."

"I'm so sorry, Dr. Stewart. I want you to know that I'm going to do whatever I can to help bring closure for you and Mary Jane."

"It's Brad, just Brad. Don't worry about calling me Dr. Stewart. I'm going to do whatever I can too, but I'm not quite sure what that is right now. My lawyers have my actions and comments pretty much scripted at the moment, and I'm letting them do their thing. There's too much at stake and I hate the fact that I'm boxed in here while the killer is roaming about scot-free."

"Hopefully not for long."

Brad nodded, but I had a feeling he didn't believe me.

"Hey, here's my cell phone number." I handed Brad my business card out of my purse. "Call me if you think of anything, or if you just want to talk." I had a feeling Brad's social circle was about to get really small. "Maybe I can bring takeout over or something."

"Sounds great, just make sure it's not Thai."

I cocked my head, not following. "Got something against a little heat?" Personally, Taiwanese chili peppers were a favorite of mine.

"Ah, no. It's the nuts. I have a peanut allergy."

"Oh man, that sucks. I'm allergic to bees and had a pretty nasty reaction this summer." Thanks to a psychotic bee keeper. "So, no Thai. Got it. And seriously, give me a call. Believe it or not, this isn't my first time helping someone navigate a murder investigation."

"Thanks, Ziva. I really do appreciate it."

"Anytime."

16

I had never been to a plastic surgeon before. In fact, I'd always been a bit judgmental toward people who wanted a little nip tuck. But the more I thought about it, I realized I could be wrong. Wasn't I in the beauty business? Didn't I want to help people feel the best about themselves? Perhaps, sometimes that meant having a bit of work done. That's not to say *I* was ready to slide under the knife, but I had gained a better understanding of why people choose to do so. Brad had left a lasting impression on me.

I sat in the rental car and thought about what had just happened. What did I know?

That I liked Brad.

No, not like that. My heart was still torn about Finn. This was more of a gut reaction, a first impression of the doctor. Brad seemed like a nice guy. I had wanted to leave the appointment ready to accuse him of murder, and now I wanted to clear his name. How messed up was that?

My phone rang and I swore to goodness gracious that if it was Finn, I was going to chuck the thing out of the window. I no longer cared if he had my stuff or not; it could all be easily replaced. I looked at the caller ID and saw that it was my dad. He was probably wondering where I was, since it was already Tuesday afternoon and we were scheduled to be back home yesterday. I wasn't doing very well in the daughter department, not keeping my parents updated. I didn't want them to worry about me, so there was no way I was sharing my recent events. I quickly answered the phone, "Hey, Dad. What's up?"

"Well, I just got off the phone with a very depressed young man." *Oh no he didn't. Finn better not have called my parents.* That was low, to bring the parents into this. "Sweet sugar, Mom's probably crocheting something."

"Just a prayer shawl," my dad said, and chuckled. "Listen, hun, Finn didn't go into any details, just that he thinks there's some miscommunication going on. He wanted me to reach out to you, make sure you're okay."

Oh, I'll reach out to him all right. Maybe in a choke hold.

"Yeah, Dad. I'm okay. I should be back home tomorrow." Or maybe the next day. I should probably have stopped telling people that I'd be home in a day or two when I was no closer to solving these murders than I was on Friday night.

"Okay, and I'm not going to pry, but I just want to say that you should talk to him."

"Dad—"

My dad interrupted me. "Just talk to him." I thought of the women on the boat and Finn eagerly posing with them. Talking with the man was the last thing I wanted to do. But then my next thought was of Dr. Stewart, and my problems seemed almost trivial compared to his. I sighed.

"Okay, Dad. I will." My dad didn't press the issue or tell me to call him right then, and I was grateful for that. That's why my dad was the best. My mom, on the other hand? Oh Lordy, she'd better not call me anytime soon.

I clicked off with my dad and stared at my phone. "What to do? What to do?" My phone rang, springing me from my thoughts. Finn. I hit answer and waited a beat before saying anything, "Hey."

Really original, I know.

"Hey."

"What's up?"

"Listen, can we please talk?"

"You got me on the phone." Okay, so maybe I was still a little hot.

"You butt, not like that."

I was silent while I debated my options. Ignore him forever, or hear him out? It was about fifty-fifty at that point.

"I'll throw in some mint chocolate-chip ice cream," Finn said in a sing-songy voice.

"How many scoops?"

"Two."

"Three," I countered, "and it'd better be a waffle cone."

"Fine. Do we have a deal?"

"You're playing dirty, but you've got yourself a deal." If things went south fast, I'd at least have ice cream to bring me comfort.

~

FINN BOUGHT TWO WAFFLE CONES, just to be safe, and we walked a-ways down from the ice cream parlor to sit on a nearby park bench.

"Okay, you have me here. Now what did you want to say?" I asked.

"First off, I love you." My eyes bored holes into him.

Playing the love card right off the bat seemed about as low as calling my parents, but I needed to keep my temper in check. Last thing I needed was to have a public quarrel with Finn. Detective Blackwell would've reveled in that tidbit.

"Don't give me that look. I do, I love you. So much that it makes me stupid sometimes. When you called me out on everything, I wasn't thinking. In fact, when Kevin put that contract in front of me, I wasn't thinking. Well, I was, but not about how it would make you feel."

Okay. He had my attention. I looked at him as if to say, "*Go on.*"

"You see, the thing is, you make me want to be better because you deserve better. You deserve more than some guy who is a part-time fishing charter captain at a bait-and-tackle shop in Port Haven. I want to be more so I can give you more. That's the type of man I want to be for you."

Gulp. "All that for little ol' me?" I went with humor because otherwise I might've cried, given how deeply Finn's words hit me.

"I'd do a lot more for you." Finn took my hand, and gosh darn it, he had me. How could he not? When he put it that way, I guess I could forgive him, but there was still the question of the girls on the boat and my unanswered calls. I couldn't let that go.

"And the girls in their bikinis? Don't think I wasn't keeping an eye on you."

"Kevin's idea."

"Uh-huh."

"Honestly, he's kind of a marketing genius, but a little sexist. He has this whole social media following of the Girls of Tampa who fish his charter. I hate to say it, but the men really like it." Of course, they did. "But I won't participate in it again, since I see how much it bothered you. I respect you."

"Did Kevin tell you not to answer your phone too?"

"No, I just wanted to have this conversation in person."

"And you never called me because...?"

"Honey, I know the way you think, and I know you needed some space. I wasn't worried about you in the least. You're a big girl. You can hold your own, which is why I gave you some space, but I have to confess ... it was killing me not talking to you."

I tried to not get caught up in his compliments and keep the conversation on task. "So, what now? You're moving to Florida? I have a business to run in Port Haven." Finn could say all the sweet nothings he wanted, but facts were facts.

"I know, and this is the selfish part of me, but I was hoping you would think about expanding your business, maybe franchising? Because, I swear to you, I'll find a way out of that contract if you can't be here with me."

I sat thinking about what Finn had said for so long that my ice cream started to melt down the cone, something that had never happened before. My instinct was to dismiss his idea as a ridiculous notion. My business was still new, and I had just agreed to take on another employee. Could I take on more risk? Was it completely foolish? Then I thought about the potential Lavish contract and saw the possibilities dance before my eyes.

"I'm not saying yes, but it could be a possibility," I conceded.

"That's good enough for me," Finn replied and then leaned in for a wowzer of a kiss. I wasn't sure which was a bigger crime, the way he kissed me or the ice cream cone that splattered on the sidewalk. Turns out, it didn't matter. I would forgive him for both.

"You're going to pay for that," I muttered between breaths.

"Babe, I'm already planning on it."

~

It didn't take long for Finn and me to start talking about the case. It turned out that Detective Blackwell hadn't been able to track him down, and I was certain that was partially fueling her suspicion of me.

"Wait, you found another dead body?" Finn asked incredulously. I had just filled him in on what happened when I'd stormed out of the hotel room.

"Mmm-hmm," I said while taking a lick off my new ice cream cone. "Sterling's, on the beach." I raised my eyebrows as if to say, "*Aren't I lucky?*"

"Looks like I'll have to go to Plan B," Finn said under his breath.

"What's that?" I asked.

"Oh, nothing, nothing," but the way he said it with a smile had me second-guessing his motives.

"And the detective has it out for you?"

"More like *us*. I'm positive you're on her radar just as much, if not more, than me. Someone told her about our little fight at the hotel and she speculated it was about killing Marissa."

"Yeah, because that makes sense."

"She's not an ace detective. I can tell that she's grasping at straws. The problem is, and I know it as much as she does, things with this case just aren't adding up. There has to be someone we're both overlooking." I gave Finn a rundown of everyone I had interviewed, leaving out how I managed a face-to-face meeting with Mr. Aldrich. I was grateful he didn't think to ask.

"You don't think Marissa's husband is involved in any way?"

"No. The problem is, everything points to him, but that's too easy. Look, his wife was cheating on him, he's a plastic surgeon—so he'd know just where to stab her—and they had a big public blow-out the day before. The list goes on. But when I met with him, I don't know, he just doesn't seem capable of that kind of atrocity. The look on his face, well, let's just say it's the look of an innocent man staring down a life sentence. He knows he's screwed, and it's not right." Honestly, I had a feeling he was going to be Detective Blackwell's new obsession. The poor man.

"What about Sterling's wife? You said she barged into the doctor's office."

"Oh yeah, she was definitely hot and thinking that Dr. Stewart murdered her husband, and his wife. Like I said, it's a conclusion that a lot of people have come to, especially the media." I had scoped out a couple of the stories online and they were painting a pretty nasty picture of Dr. Stewart and Marissa's marriage. He was portrayed as a jealous husband, and her the up-and-coming starlet. I didn't consider Marissa a starlet by any stretch of imagination, but it was the type of story the entertainment industry sucked up with a flavor straw. It didn't take much to captivate the minds of the American public.

"Anyone else?" Finn asked.

"Oh my gosh, I totally forgot about Claire. She's the other DSC host, the redhead. I don't know if you saw her or not. Anyway, both she and Marissa were going after the same job at the same time. She claimed that Marissa was a nasty, backstabbing coworker, and she was all Little Miss

Innocent, getting out of town because she was frightened, but I'm not so sure I should've bought that."

"Where is Claire now?"

"I have no idea. I actually ran into her back home." Finn cocked his head. "Yeah, I forgot to mention that I drove to Port Haven and back on Sunday. Long story." Finn opened and closed his mouth like he wished to argue, but thought against it. For once, he was being smart.

"What's your gut say?" Finn asked.

"I don't know. There are still too many loose ends and open questions. For one, I have no idea how Sterling died. For all we know, it could've been natural causes." I wasn't buying that, but I had to admit it was a possibility. There hadn't been any visual markings on his body to indicate that he had been shot or stabbed. No clues to tip me off one way or the other. "Another theory that I've kind of tossed around is that maybe he committed suicide."

"Why would you think that?"

"I'm not sure exactly, but I was thinking that maybe after Marissa and Dr. Stewart got into that fight, she was having second thoughts about being with Sterling. Dr. Stewart never said anything, but I heard from the CEO that Marissa knew she wasn't getting the prime-time spot. So, the 'power couple' vision she had was never going to come to fruition, not at DSC. If that was her motive for the affair, then I can see her calling it off. She had more prestige being the doctor's wife than being Sterling's arm candy. Maybe that was too much for Sterling to take."

"You're definitely on to something. If that's the case, though, I wonder if there's a suicide note." That was one angle I hadn't given much thought to. He obviously didn't leave one at home, or his wife wouldn't have been barging into Dr. Stewart's office to accuse him of murder. I thought of where else Sterling would have left one, if one existed. All I came up with was his office. I was sure the police had already searched it, but what if they missed something? I really wanted to take a look for myself.

"How the heck are we going to break into DSC headquarters?" I kept my voice low, but it didn't really matter because no one was paying any attention.

"I could do it. You could provide cover and text me if anything came up."

Okay, I know that might've been the smart thing to do, but I didn't want to miss out on any of the action. Besides, I knew the lay of the land, not Finn.

"You think it's worth it? The risk, I mean." I'm assuming the police searched every inch of his office. It's not like a suicide note was going to be left in his desk drawer. I had thought of that once before; but the more I analyzed it, the more I realized it was pointless to search Sterling's office.

"Does committing suicide void life insurance?"

"I think so. Why? Where are you going with this?"

"Hear me out. If I were going to kill myself, I'd definitely want to leave a note to let my close family and friends know why, but that doesn't mean I'd want the entire world to know. Leaving a public suicide note would do just that. Especially being a celebrity. I wouldn't want my deepest darkest secrets to be the eight o'clock breaking news.

"So, what would you do?

"Email it." It was the most basic solution I could think of.

"Whose email do you want to hack into?" I gave some thought before answering. It wouldn't have done Sterling any good to email Marissa, seeing she was already dead, and quite possibly at his hands. I couldn't see him emailing a confession to her husband either. Surely, he would have taken that immediately to the police. The only person who would have kept his suicide a secret would've been his wife, Mary Jane, and I told Finn as much.

"Okay, let's do it," Finn replied.

I don't know if I should have been more alarmed or relieved that my beau was all gung-ho on hacking into somebody's email address, but I fell in love with him a little bit more after that statement. Still, he did get a couple of raised eyebrows from me. "I love your eagerness and all, and this might come as a surprise to you, but I can't even hack into my own email account, let alone someone else's." Seriously, I forget my password all the time.

"I can." He averted his eyes downward.

"Come again?"

He blew out a big puff of air and looked back up at me. "Let's just say, I wasn't always as virtuous as I am now."

"Ooh, I'm sure there's a good story behind those words, but I'm going to let you save it for another day. Right now, I want you to walk me through this whole hacking process."

While I finished my ice cream cone, Finn gave me the rundown. I learned that there are primarily two ways to hack into someone's email. One is phishing, which requires creating fake email login pages that mirror the legitimate ones, and stealing the information as soon as the user enters it. It was the more sophisticated option, but it also required the most development time and came with some serious legal ramifications. I had escaped jail time twice this week and I didn't want to chance it again. However, it was an option that remained on the table, but not our go-to just yet.

The other option Finn mentioned was a method called key logging. The way he described it, key logging is basically a software secretly installed on the user's computer that records every keystroke the person types in. The best part was that it could be installed remotely, and it was virtually undetectable while working. The program then uploads the key log to a private server that only we could access online. I left the details up to Finn, as I understood it was a bit more complicated than that, especially getting it installed on her computer and what to do with the key log once we had it. Finn started to go in depth about a buddy of his who could convert the program file to attach to a photo, so when she opened her email and clicked on it, the program would automatically install. My eyes started to glaze over. I didn't understand all that technical stuff and decided to leave it entirely up to him. I sat back while he made some phone calls and got everything "all set," whatever that meant. Fingers crossed, we would strike gold.

17

We decided to take a little road trip after the ice cream shop and ended up at one of Finn's favorite places—a pawn shop.

One of Finn's hidden talents is the ability to sniff out a pawn shop anywhere. But it doesn't stop there. Flea markets, garage sales—they're all fair game. He's a master at finding second-hand junk. In fact, we both have a love for second-hand goods. However, I prefer antiques, as the owner of the shop below my apartment will attest to. Kathleen knows my style and I find something to love every time I go in there, especially jewelry.

As Finn and I stood in the pawn shop, it wasn't jewelry that caught my eye this time, but a beautiful perfume bottle. It was a perfectly round, blue-green glass globe. The color was like sea glass with the gold top and ivory spray tassel. So classy. I really wanted it for my collection. Maybe I'd create something a little bit more sensuous to fill it with.

"Babe, look at this," Finn said to me.

I walked over to the display case next to him and peered

down at a gold necklace that I'd recognize anywhere. I forgot all about the perfume bottle.

"My cross!" I touched my neck. I had no idea how the piece had ended up in a pawn shop outside Tampa, but I didn't care. I just wanted to have it around my neck once more.

"Are you folks interested in something?" An older man with thick-rimmed glasses and patchy white stubble walked the length of the display case to meet us.

I didn't even attempt to follow the golden rule of "playing it cool" at that moment. I lost all composure and blurted out, "This is mine. I want it back," pointing through the glass at the necklace.

"Well now, if I had a dollar for every time I heard that," the man said dryly.

"I'm serious, I don't know where you got this, but it was stolen from me last week." It was the only plausible explanation. The alternative being that I dropped it, someone found it, and then hocked it here, which was even harder to believe than someone stealing it and fencing it.

"Listen, lady, I don't know anything about any stolen necklace, but if you're interested in this piece, you're in luck because it's on sale."

I glared hard at the weasel. "Or I could call the cops. Maybe they could look around, see if anything else is hot."

The man looked around the store and I followed his eyes. He stared at a pretty abstract piece in the corner.

"That painting right there perhaps?" I questioned.

The man's eyes snapped back to mine and I smiled. I had him and he knew it.

"Who should we call? Detective Blackwell? Do you know her?"

"Fine, take the necklace and get out of here. Don't ever

come back." The man tossed the necklace across the counter and I caught it with one hand.

"Trust me, not a problem."

We were out of there a second later.

"Babe, that was hot." I rolled my eyes at Finn, but accepted his hand.

"So, riddle me this, Batman, how the heck did my necklace get there?" I asked him on our walk back to the truck.

"I have no clue. I'm just glad you got it back."

"I know, me too, but I have a feeling there's more to it than that. Do you think the two events are connected?" I tended to work things out in my head but didn't always explain them to others as clearly.

Finn's brows gathered. "Which two?"

"The person who stole my necklace, and the one I saw creeping around Marissa's dressing room Saturday morning."

"The what? You didn't tell me anything about this."

"Wait, what?" I couldn't believe that I had forgotten to tell Finn about DSC's very own cat burglar. I gave him a quick rundown of what I had seen.

"I forgot to ask Brad if anything had been stolen, particularly of the jewelry variety, off Marissa's body."

"Are you thinking whoever murdered Marissa came back Saturday morning for evidence?"

"Not evidence. Jewelry. A gorgeous diamond necklace."

~

IT TURNED out the best part of breaking up was indeed making up, which we did that night. A lot. I smiled at my sleeping beau, with his messy blond bedroom hair and his body wrapped up in the only sheet left on the bed, and tiptoed off for a shower. We decided that our first order of business would be to visit Sterling's wife. With her, I was braced for the unexpected. Whoever would barge into a place of business and accuse someone of murder might not have a grip on their emotions. I had no idea if she had worked through that anger or if Finn and I were going to walk right into it.

Now that Finn and I were back together, I had access to my original wardrobe. I toweled off and stepped into my off-the-shoulder black and red flowered dress that I had originally worn when arriving to DSC's studios. I pulled my hair up into a messy twist and wore a simple pair of diamond studs in my ears, and my cross was back safely around my neck. I wanted to look professional yet approachable. Finn was already dressed and just about ready to go when I stepped back out into the room. He had opted for the same tan shorts and his white short-sleeved button down from yesterday. All he needed to do was brush his teeth. Men had it so easy.

"What?" Finn looked at me as I assessed his wardrobe.

"Just debating the unfairness of our genders."

He nodded in agreement. "It is quite unfair, but I do like it when you get all done up." Finn stood behind me and bent to nibble on my ear.

"Stop it! We need to go. Now!" Truthfully, he probably could've persuaded me to stay a little while longer, but I really didn't want to have to redo my makeup.

~

STERLING'S OCEANSIDE home was situated in South Tampa. The Spanish-style home featured impressive archways, wrought iron and dark wood accents, and a red brick driveway dotted with palm trees. I could have lived there, for sure.

Finn accompanied me to the door and I rang the bell. It took Mary Jane less than a minute to answer. She acted like a perfectly sane individual by saying hello and smiling. I took that as a good sign. Once again, I was struck by how beautiful she was. Even with her red-rimmed eyes and makeup-free face, she had the look of natural beauty that my clients coveted. I wondered in that moment why Sterling had strayed. I couldn't help but ponder the details of their marriage. Of course, I wasn't about to ask a grieving widow about that, but if anyone—like the network's chatty receptionist—wanted to dish on it, I would gladly listen. Mary Jane looked at me expectantly and it took me a minute to find my manners. "I'm sorry. My name is Ziva Diaz, and this is my boyfriend, Finn." Finn smiled at me all funny-like when I introduced him that way. It took forever for me to get used to the title. Even now I didn't use it all that often, but I had already made up my mind that that was about to change.

"I'm," I tried to find a way to say this politely, "I'm the one who found your husband's body on the beach. Can we come inside and talk to you for a minute?"

Mary Jane hesitated for a moment before holding the door open and inviting us in.

The house looked busy, with other family members milling around. In the front sitting room, a group of people congregated around photo albums and shoeboxes full of photos. A man, who appeared to be in his forties, was busy scanning photos into a flash drive for what I assumed would be the slideshow for the funeral.

"I'm sorry, I should've realized you'd be busy with family.

We can come back later." I looked to Finn for confirmation and he was seconding what I had just said.

"MJ, who is it?" the man in the living room asked.

"Just some friends." MJ looked over her shoulder and waved him off before turning back to us and saying, "No, that's okay. I have some questions for you, too." We followed MJ down the tiled floor into her kitchen. The Spanish style flowed throughout the house with the use of warm tones and bright pops of color, like the blue accent tiles on the backsplash. The kitchen table was teeming with plates of cookies and appetizers, fruit baskets, and flowers. It appeared that the well-wishers had been paying their condolences in full force. I eyed the lilies on the counter and prayed they wouldn't make my allergies kick in.

"Tea?" MJ asked.

"No, I'm good, thank you," I replied.

"Here, let me get that for you." Finn took the red kettle from MJ and filled it with water and then placed it on the gas stove's back burner.

"Like I said, I'm really sorry to just show up like this," I said.

"That's okay. Honestly, we're all just waiting around here for news. The police haven't told me much."

"I know, Detective Blackwell—"

"—is not a nice woman," MJ finished for me. "Not very sensitive, anyway." MJ shuddered and I could only imagine what the detective had accused her of.

"Don't worry. It's not just you. She came on pretty hard with me too, well, us," I said, motioning to Finn.

"Why you?"

"Because, not only did I find your husband's body, but Marissa's as well, and Finn was with me for part of it."

"I can't even imagine." I nodded my head to acknowledge her statement.

"Anyway, let's just say I haven't been impressed with Detective Blackwell and I want to make sure that justice is served, to allow your husband to rest in peace," I said.

MJ got all teary eyed and blew out a breath to steady herself. I looked uncomfortably at Finn. He knew crying gave me the heeby jeebies.

"Thanks for that. This whole thing is just so ... well, I'm not sure which emotion to lead with. I loved my husband, so very much." And with that statement, a tear did slip down her cheek. I looked frantically for a tissue to put the kibosh on that. Finn beat me to it.

"Thank you." MJ took another deep breath and said, "So, what did you want to know?"

"I don't want to be insensitive, but I'm trying to make sense of what happened."

"No, I understand. We all want answers. If you're going to ask me about Marissa, the answer is I don't know."

"You didn't know he was seeing her?" I thought Finn worded their relationship nicely, given the way Tess had described it to me.

"Right. I knew he was impressed by her, just based off dinner table conversation. He was excited about work again. He had grown tired of Tess years ago and was looking forward to something new. He seemed happy, recharged."

"He was, for sure, staying with the network?" I knew Tess had said he was, but wasn't sure if she knew what she was talking about. She wasn't necessarily thinking clearly.

"Oh yes. He had just renewed his contract for another three years."

"And he thought he would be working with Marissa?" Finn asked.

"He seemed sure of it. Why?"

"Well, another girl was hired the same time as Marissa, a girl named Claire," I said. I watched MJ search her memory for a moment and decided to help her out. "Kind of petite, long red hair?"

"No, I don't think I know her," she supplied.

So, we knew that Sterling's contract had been renewed and that he had been planning on working with Marissa. I filed that information away.

"You were at the gala Friday night, weren't you?" I wanted to see if her answer matched what I already knew.

"Yes, of course. I try and make it every year. It's so great the way the network gives back to the community. I know the agencies that receive the donations are very appreciative.

"Did anything seem off with your husband?" I was still trying to work out the whole murder-suicide angle, but I didn't want MJ to know that.

"Nothing that stands out. We met some friends for a couple of Manhattans and then had our driver drop us off at DSC. In fact, Sterling was in a wonderful mood. His famous charm was on full display. We were having a wonderful time. It wasn't until we were all ushered into the ballroom, and word got around that Marissa had been murdered, that he became upset. I had never seen my husband so distraught before. I thought it was because of the manner of her death and her being a good friend of his. I hadn't expected the full truth." Her eyes lowered.

"When did you find out?" Finn asked.

"That they were having an affair? From *Entertainment Now*." My heart sank for the poor woman. "That Cee Cee Thomas came knocking on my door, asking for a statement. I had no idea what she was talking about until I turned on the TV and watched the coverage for myself."

Ouch.

"What do you think happened?" I asked.

MJ was lost in thought, but my question snapped her back to the present. "I think Dr. Stewart killed them." Her misty eyes turned sharp, and I saw a flash of the anger that I knew simmered just below the surface.

"Can I ask why you're so set on it being him?"

"If not him, then who? My Sterling certainly wasn't involved." I loved the way she referred to her husband as "My Sterling," as if he had been the model spouse. She was protective of him, nonetheless, and I was sure she wouldn't be too pleased to know what I was thinking, which was that her husband killed himself in desperation. Having been dumped cold by Marissa and faced with the monotony of life, he just couldn't stand it anymore. It might sound like a bit of a stretch, but it was the best I had. Hopefully Finn's hacking buddy would give us some evidence to go off of.

"Dr. Stewart is a man of many talents. Holding his temper isn't one of them. I've seen his anger explode a time or two, and it's not pretty." MJ's comment caught my attention. I saw a glimpse of something when I confessed to the doctor about my true intentions for the office visit, but I hadn't been able to quite put my finger on it. Maybe that was it. I thought about directing a lot of questions back toward Dr. Stewart and why MJ specifically suspected him, but I knew what her answer would probably be: the money, the anger, his reputation. I had heard the motives delivered in the media, sounding like a broken record. I wondered how the doctor with the kind eyes was holding up.

MJ never picked up on my train of thought, and I wasn't about to clue her in. She was clearly set in her theory, which also meant that Sterling hadn't left a suicide note lying around, or one that she would tell me about. I had a fervent desire to search their house, but I had no idea how I would pull that off, not with family milling around.

I excused myself to go to the restroom, figuring that was as good as it would get, but I wasn't expecting to find much. It wasn't like there would be a suicide note in the bathroom vanity. However, what I did find was enough beauty creams and lotions to stock the shelves of my store for weeks, in addition to some vials of off-brand Botox and the woman's own personal selection of needles. I was wrong. MJ's beauty wasn't as natural as it appeared to be. She was clearly vested in her appearance. I imagine living life in the limelight, one had to be. I had never had a desire to be famous, and I clearly did not possess one now.

Finn had picked up the conversation in my absence, and I heard him asking MJ about what part of upstate New York she was from. Apparently, my beau had spent some time there in his youth.

"That's an awesome photo," Finn was saying as I rejoined them. A few of MJ's family members had gathered in the kitchen and brought a stack of photos with them. I scooted next to Finn and looked over his shoulder. "Wow, that is beautiful. Where is that? Niagara Falls?"

"Have you ever been there?" Finn asked me.

"No, can't say I have, but I've always wanted to go. They look breathtaking."

"We'll have to change that," Finn said with a wink as he flipped to the next photo. It was one of MJ in a white silk slip dress, little stephanotises braided into her long blonde hair. Sterling's arm was linked with hers, he in a cream-colored suit and barefoot just like her. It was their wedding photo. From the condition of the 4 x 4 photo, I guessed it was circa 1970-something. It was a candid shot of the two walking, looking at each other.

I didn't call the photo out to MJ. Personally, I thought the change in conversation had been good for her. Some color had returned to her cheeks and her eyes were now completely dry. I didn't want to loop her back into depression.

"You about ready?" I asked Finn.

"Yeah, let's go."

We were getting ready to take leave when MJ turned to me. "And Ziva?" I had forgotten that she had wanted to ask me something as well. "This is probably inappropriate, but I was just wondering, well, if you could tell me anything about Sterling. The police have kept all the details away from me and I just want to make sure that he ... looked okay." I stared at the woman, unsure of how to respond. Saying "*I found your husband face down in the sand*" didn't seem like something that would've gone over well. I went with a generalization. "He looked okay. Nothing gruesome or anything like that. Honestly, I can't even tell you how he died."

MJ nodded her head. "Thank you for that. The nightmares, I can't quite explain what I've seen in my sleep."

I could understand. Sometimes the unknown was worse than the known. The mind could be cruel like that.

"Well, that was depressing," Finn said when we got back in his truck.

"I know."

"I'm going to say that it's a big fat negative on her being the killer."

"I'm in agreement with you there. The problem is, that's the same conclusion I've come to after everyone I've interviewed."

"Who does that leave?" Finn asked.

"I don't know. It seems something is missing. Unless it's

just the whole murder-suicide thing after all. But without a suicide note, I'm not sure how to get Detective Blackwell to believe that, or even point the case in that direction. For Dr. Stewart's case, I really hope the evidence leads that way. If there's anything hinky found, it's all going to fall on him."

18

"Let's take a break."

"What?" I was withdrawn and looked at Finn like he was crazy. How could we stop now?

"It would do you good to step away for the afternoon."

I shifted my weight from foot to foot to think about it. "What type of break did you have in mind?"

"I don't know, the beach?" I shook my head. No way was I relaxing on the beach right now. "Okay, not the beach. How about lunch, a little shopping, just you know, go back to what our original plans were for Saturday afternoon. A little *us* time."

"You hate shopping."

"For girlie things, but maybe there's some cool stuff downtown." I hadn't had a chance to explore the downtown shopping district, and I had to admit that his idea had some appeal. I wasn't sure we could salvage this vacation but it was worth a shot.

We ended up eating at this little French bistro where every dish on the menu, make that "le menu," had an accent in its title. It was a point-to-order kind of menu.

"What looks good, babe?"

I was leaning more toward wine and cheese pairings, seeing I'd just finished an enormous ice cream cone. I pointed a couple out to him.

"Do you want to grab an appetizer to go with it?"

"Yeah, we can do that."

Our waiter stopped by to take our order and my mouth dropped open when Finn started speaking in French. The waiter smiled in surprise, but switched from English to French with ease. Quite pleased with themselves, the two men conversed for a minute or two, laughing like old chums.

Meanwhile, I shut my mouth to keep from looking like an idiot, and smiled politely as if I knew what they were saying. Finn switched back to English, "So the Fourme d'Ambert and Époisses for the cheese selection and the Terrine à la mode Landaus and gnocchi à la Parisienne for apps?" he asked me.

"Sounds great."

"And a bottle of what? Burgundy?"

"Perfect." Honestly, I had no idea if that paired well with the meal, but the waiter pumped his head with approval, so it must have been a good choice.

The waiter left us, and I looked at Finn like he had sprouted two heads. "You speak French?!" I asked when the waiter was out of earshot. "How did I not know this?"

"One of my many talents." I thought I knew all the man's talents, but Finn had managed to surprise me yet again.

The waiter brought out our first selection and my mouth melted with the first bite. He had me at Époisses. I'd snack on this "stinky" cheese any day. Especially if it was served with the same crunchy baguette and fig compote.

About two hours later, our meal was complete and I was

fully sated. I no longer cared about Tess or anyone else besides the man I was dining with. If Detective Blackwood wanted to focus on Dr. Stewart, so be it.

Finn and I left the restaurant and walked hand in hand around South Tampa, strolling along the boutique and palm tree-lined streets. It was like Port Haven, only more luxurious. We walked past a vacant storefront and I paused for longer than I'd intended.

"So, can you see it?"

"Hmm?" I was still lost in my thoughts, but I knew what Finn meant. I tried to brush off his comment, but yeah, I could see it. The atmosphere felt right. Maybe Izzy's intuition had started to rub off on me, or maybe that crystal she gave me was to blame, but I was definitely feeling some good vibrations. Still, I played devil's advocate. "But just because I can see it, doesn't mean it can happen."

"Babe, if anyone can make it happen, I know you can."

Well, maybe not just me. It might take a couple of lucrative deals, and Izzy would have to be interested in managing the Port Haven store full time, but wasn't that what she was already doing?

I turned around to stare at the open storefront. I had no idea how much rent cost or what the demographics of the area was like, but I was already envisioning the layout inside. Finn kissed my head. "Come on, there's something else I want to show you."

Our next stop required us to get in the car. On the drive to the marina, Finn talked on and on about the new boat he'd be captaining. I thought it was only fair to let him ramble on. He was helping me realize my dreams, so the least I could do was let him bask in his new success too. I had spent my fair share of time at marinas with Finn. It was pretty much the life of girlfriends and wives of marina men.

I gazed at rows upon rows of docks and boat slips. However, where Murphy's Bait & Tackle was weathered, this marina was polished. Commercial vessels weren't taking off from here. This was all residential and recreational.

"I thought you were going to show me your new boat?" Finn had led me down the dock toward the more residential boats.

"I am, I am, but first I wanted to show you something really quick." Finn took me by the hand and led me all the way down the dock toward the far side of the marina. "What do you think?" he asked, coming to a stop in front of a beautiful white houseboat. The wooden vessel looked like it had more deck space than one would ever need for a fishing charter, and I could easily make out the staircase leading to rooms below.

"It's lovely," I replied. The boat wasn't new, but it had charm. I could see why Finn was drawn to it and I had a feeling I knew what he had in mind. "You're planning on renovating this, aren't you?"

"Bingo. Just picture it—with the deck space like this, you can put a hot tub on it." I wasn't sure about the hot tub, but I could appreciate his creativity. "And with open space over here, you could easily have an outdoor couch that wraps around, maybe even a little bar area. Seriously, this open deck is about fifteen feet wide and the boat is fifty feet long. There's some serious space up here. Come on board with me."

I looked around before accepting Finn's hand. "Are you sure we should be getting on this thing?"

"Yeah, absolutely. I've already had a couple of conversations with the current owner." From the deck, I could easily understand Finn's vision. There really was enough space to fit a hot tub and bar and a couch up there. "Here's the best part. Look at the space below deck." I followed Finn down the steps and was surprised to see how tall the ceilings were and how much space was below. The only time I'd been in the bottom of a boat, I'd found a dead body, so this was much more pleasant. The core was a bit dated—1980s at least—but just like above, the lower deck also had potential.

"Just picture it, babe. We can easily replace these appliances over here with a full-sized refrigerator, stove, sink, everything ... just like a custom RV. Then down the hall here are two bedrooms. All I have to do is replace the wood paneling with something a bit nicer-looking, and replace the floors. We could add some bamboo floors, maybe maple cabinets, or even birch." Finn was daydreaming and I found it adorable. I had no doubt that the man would be able to renovate this boat. I had seen him work wonders with his apartment. If he could turn that empty shell of a building into a modern-day living space, I was sure he could do the same with this boat.

"And I think we should live here," Finn said, turning around to take my hand and gauge my reaction.

"Wait, what?"

"Think about it. It's the perfect solution. It's a boat and a house. I could dock it at the marina in Port Haven, or we could keep it here in Tampa. We'd have a home wherever we go."

Okay, I liked the sound of that and all. "But what about Captain Jack?" I couldn't see how my little dog could live on a houseboat.

"There's a dog run right next to the marina. It's part of the services that come with the boat slip. Heck, a dog lives on this boat right now." Finn motioned to the oversize food and water bowl tucked underneath the kitchen counter. By the size of those bowls, I guessed it was a much bigger dog than my miniature poodle.

"I'm not asking you to marry me—"

"—Yes," I interrupted him.

"Yes? Yes, what?"

"I want to marry you." That revelation didn't freak me out, make me want to run away, or act like a total psycho the way it would've even a couple of months ago.

"You want to marry me? But I didn't ask you!"

"What, are you saying, you don't want to marry me?" I gave Finn the eye.

"Ugh, you are such a butt." And then Finn did something I didn't expect. He got down on one knee and pulled a little black box out of his cargo shorts pocket. My heart skipped a beat, but in a good way.

"Ziva Marie Diaz, I love you with every ounce of my being, even when you drive me crazy. Will you do me the honor of marrying me?"

"YES!" I held out my shaky hand for Finn to slide on the ring.

The last time a man proposed to me, I was more in love with the ring than the man. This time, the ring was just a nice bonus. Finn knew I had a thing for colored diamonds and his choice of ring did not disappoint. The antique cushion-cut pink diamond was surrounded by a halo of tiny white diamonds, all set in rose gold. Did I ever mention I have a thing for pink? Especially when it comes to diamonds and champagne. The ring sparkled brilliantly back at me.

"My dad!" I suddenly thought back to tradition and felt a pang of guilt.

"He knows."

"What?!"

"I asked him about a month ago."

"You did not."

"Honey, I've known I wanted to marry you for a while, so I let your parents know."

"Ah, that would explain how adamant he was about me making amends with you."

Finn chuckled and gave me that irresistible grin. "He may have been privy to some classified information."

I smiled back and wrapped him in a hug. "I love you."

"I love you too."

I looked around the deck of the boat, down to my ring, and back at Finn. I felt so blessed I thought I'd cry.

"We need to go before I get all emotional on you," I said, trying to will back my happy tears.

"You're so cute when you cry."

"I am not!" Once I started, I knew I would melt into a blubbering mess.

"Okay, we can go. How do you think we should celebrate?"

"Oh, I can think of a few ideas," I said with a wink.

As we left the dock, I glanced over my shoulder once more. Yeah, this all felt right, but my happiness was short-lived when I thought of Dr. Stewart and Mary Jane both grieving over their deceased spouses. One would suppose that maybe they shouldn't grieve so hard, seeing that their spouses had cheated on them, but I'd found that the heart didn't work that way. Of course, I wouldn't have to worry about that, not anymore. If I ever found out that Finn cheated on me and we were married, I'd probably be the one to kill him. Just kidding, mostly. But I can guarantee I would be a prime suspect. I understood why the police, make that Detective Blackwood, had zoomed in so tightly on Dr. Stewart after not being able to get anything to stick on me.

FINN and I stopped by a party store to pick up a bottle of bubbly to celebrate our new engagement. Pink bubbly, of course. Unfortunately, we never did get a chance until much later to pop the cork as Cee Cee called me, frantically shouting into the phone, "Someone tried to kill Dr. Stewart at his office. I'm headed there now."

It might've just been a coincidence, but at that same moment, a firetruck and an ambulance whizzed by us, headed the same direction as Dr. Stewart's office. You know in those cop movies where a call comes in from dispatch and the officers jump in their car? That was Finn and me right at that minute. If we'd had a portable siren, I would have slapped that sucker on the roof of the car in a heartbeat.

"Turn left," I instructed Finn. I was too anxious to drive. The directions ended up being pointless because we were, in fact, following the emergency vehicles. They pulled into Dr. Stewart's parking lot a second before we did. Out front, a handful of witnesses were shuffling around, looking confused and slightly scared. Cee Cee popped up shortly thereafter, along with a couple of local news stations. *Hold the phone, is that CNN over there?!*

I looked around the building for any sign of what had just happened. No one was screaming, and I didn't see any smoke, so it couldn't have been something major.

Kelly, Dr. Stewart's receptionist, was front and center trying to control the crowd. Finn and I walked up to her and asked how we could help.

"What's going on? I heard there's been an accident?" I wasn't sure how else to word it, having no idea what had happened.

"I'm not really sure, but someone tried to kill Dr. Stewart."

"What do you mean?"

"We were having a food day in the office and, I don't know, but it looks like someone slipped some sort of peanut into one or all of the dishes."

"Oh my goodness, are you sure it wasn't an accident?"

"No way, we all know how severe Dr. Stewart's allergy is. In fact, all of us make everything from scratch and are very diligent about preventing cross-contamination. No store-bought stuff here. This was definitely deliberate."

"Is he going to be okay?"

"Katie is with him now. She gave him his injection and hooked him up to oxygen right away. His other nurse got a breathing treatment ready, and I called 911 and came outside to wait for them."

I looked over at Finn and knew he was wondering the same thing. Who would want to kill Dr. Stewart? Off the top of my head—*Mary Jane.* She had barged into his office and threatened him earlier in the week. Was she really crazy enough to kill someone? The other possibility that came to mind was Marissa's parents. Brad had mentioned how much they despised him. Parents do a lot of crazy things for their kids. I wondered if it was possible for Marissa's mother or father to attempt to kill their son-in-law. Yet another twist to this already confusing mystery.

19

I wasn't sure what I'd expected Mr. and Mrs. Morrison's house to look like, but this wasn't it. I got out of Finn's truck and shut the door, surveying the doublewide in front of me.

The Morrisons had a postage stamp-sized front yard, with rows of similar-styled homes all stacked down the road together. A navy-blue Buick Century was parked under the carport. White flower boxes overflowed with red and orange flowers, some of them marigolds, or so I thought. My flower IQ is pretty pathetic, even after spending time learning about plants' homeopathic characteristics, thanks to my friend Vicki, who taught classes at the conservatory. Right now, if it didn't have some promise in the skincare community, I was clueless.

The home's heavy wooden door was already open. It was a cool day for South Florida, with the temperature only promising to be seventy, and the residents seemed to be taking advantage of it by turning off the air conditioning and letting in some fresh air.

Finn and I walked up to the porch and he rapped on the screen door. A woman with curly red hair, sporting an old-fashioned apron, answered the front door.

"Good afternoon and God bless, how may I help you?"

I looked to Finn to take the lead. Like the house, the picture this woman portrayed was so far removed from my expectations that I was speechless.

"Hi, Mrs. Morrison. My name is Finn Hudson and this is my fiancée, Ziva Diaz." Finn couldn't help but smile when he said the word fiancée, and I may have sported a goofy grin in return, before remembering where we were. "Ziva here knew your daughter and we heard what happened. We know you two were close and we wanted to see if we could help in any way." I wasn't sure if Mrs. Morrison would buy it. After all, who knew how many people had been knocking on her door recently, but she opened the screen and invited us in anyway.

Her home was as neat as a pin, with throw pillows placed on the sofa just so. The carpet had marks from the vacuum cleaner, in perfect horizontal passes. There wasn't a speck of dust to be seen, or a magazine out of place. The woman was even wearing high heels for cripes sake, and I could see the pink-colored ruffles of her dress fan out from underneath her apron. She escorted us through her living room to her kitchen directly behind it.

"Wow." I hadn't been able to keep my thoughts to myself. It was like a bakery back there. Six pies took up the entire kitchen table, cooling on metal racks. Her countertops were covered in parchment paper with dozens upon dozens of cookies lined up, some with chocolate chips and some waiting to be frosted. And still she had room for twenty or so cupcakes, topped with chocolate frosting and multicolored sprinkles. My stomach rumbled at just the thought of getting to taste one.

"You haven't by chance been about delivering any of this, have you?" Finn asked Mrs. Morrison.

She looked at him as if he were crazy. With wide eyes she responded, "Delivering them? These are for my daughter's funeral." A sob escaped when she said the word funeral, but she quickly recovered. "As Ziva here probably knows, my daughter had a major sweet tooth. I thought, what better way to honor her than to fill her memorial with dozens of desserts." Of course, I didn't know that. Maybe if I had, Marissa and I wouldn't have gotten off to such a bad start. I was also thinking I might need to crash Marissa's memorial service later. Shame on me, I know.

"Do you need any help?" I asked, looking around at the display. The timer on the oven beeped and Mrs. Morrison zipped over to remove a batch of brownies.

"No, that's okay. I've got it. Mr. Morrison will be home soon to help me finish, and then we're taking everything over to the church."

I knew I had to tread carefully here, but I wondered if Mrs. Morrison's impression of Brad was really as bad as he thought it was. I tested the waters with, "I ran into Marissa's husband—"

"—Murderer! Mark my words: He is going to spend an eternity with the devil." Mrs. Morrison had a spatula in her hand and was pointing it right at my chest. I took a step back. Yes, Brad had been correct.

"Have you had a chance to talk with him? It's just, he seems devastated."

"It's all an act. Don't let him fool you. It was always an act with Brad; that's why Marissa was leaving him. Her father and I couldn't have been happier. If only we could have prevented the wedding in the first place." Mrs. Morrison closed her eyes and I took another step back, waiting for the waterworks, but they never came. "I'll spend the rest of my life regretting losing my daughter to that man."

"Someone tried to kill him today," Finn added. I caught the look in her eyes at the same time he did. I swear she almost smiled, and I wasn't sure what to make of it. I then wondered where Mr. Morrison had been off to. Maybe he was the one who had snuck the contaminated food into the doctor's office. It would've been a clever way to kill someone with a low chance of being caught, that's for sure.

"Well, I see that you're busy. We'll get out of your hair. We just wanted to stop by and offer our condolences." Mrs. Morrison didn't keep us and she didn't offer a cookie to-go either, but you could bet Finn and I would be stopping by a bakery before driving off too far.

~

I ENDED up going with a tuxedo cupcake, a frosted sugar cookie, and a chunk of peanut butter fudge. Finn ordered all that and more—yet another reason to love the man. We took our goodies and found a shaded spot outside the bakery to sit and indulge in our treats.

"Should I grab the champagne?"

My eyes lit up and that was all the encouragement Finn needed. He popped back into the bakery to request a couple of Styrofoam cups and then disappeared back to his truck for a minute. When he came back, he had two cups full of my favorite pink bubbly, and no one else was the wiser.

"Cheers, babe. Love you."

"Love you too." I accepted the kiss and took a sip.

"Pink champagne, chocolate, a nice little bling on my finger. You know I'm pretty much in heaven, right?"

"Ha, I'll have to remember that next time you're mad at me."

"No one said love was cheap," I joked.

"You're worth it."

"Stop it before you make me blush, or pull you away for a quickie." Finn looked pleasantly surprised at my offer.

"See, I told you I knew how to make you happy too." We may have been trying to solve a murder, but there was always time for flirting.

Finn cleared his throat. "So, what did you make of Mrs. Morrison?" he asked, biting into his tuxedo cupcake. The chocolate cupcakes dipped in ganache and then topped with white cream frosting were his favorite, and I was already picturing us serving them at our wedding. I had to stop myself for a minute. We had just gotten engaged a couple of hours ago and here I was making wedding plans.

"We have to have these at the wedding," Finn said.

Whew! I laughed. "I was just thinking the same thing."

We shared a moment and I was about to bring up possible wedding details. *Do we want a spring wedding? Maybe an exotic destination instead? Christmas-themed?* To say that I was a bit excited about becoming Mrs. Finn Hudson was an understatement.

I thankfully was able to get my brain back on track. "But, back to your question. Mrs. Morrison seemed a bit mentally unstable, right?"

"So, you're not ruling her out?"

"Not ruling her out, but I would think—and this is without even meeting the man—that maybe all of her baking inspired her husband to deliver something nefarious to Dr. Stewart's office."

"I hadn't thought of that, but you may be onto something. Or, they could have worked together."

"Very true."

"The other person I still have on my list is Mary Jane."

"I know, but that would be pretty bold of her. She already busted into the doctor's office earlier this week. Unless she doesn't think people are smart enough to put two and two together."

"You want to try talking to her again?"

"No, and unless she feels like confessing, or has peanut butter smeared all over her clothes, I don't see how we are going to get any information out of her."

Just then, Finn's phone vibrated in his pocket and he retrieved it to look at his text messages.

"Looks like my guy came through for us." Finn showed me his screen. On it was a username and password.

"Is that Mary Jane's?"

Finn nodded.

"Let's head back to the hotel and log in to see what we can find," I said.

"I have a better idea."

Finn did drive us back to the hotel, but only to run upstairs and grab my laptop. He then hopped back into the truck and drove around until stopping in the parking lot of a big box electronics store.

"Are you going to fill me in here?" I asked Finn.

"We want to make it as hard as possible for someone to trace the hacking to us. If we use the hotel's Wi-Fi and Mary Jane finds out, it wouldn't be too hard for her to discover that it was you, or at least cause the police to consider you further, because you're a guest there, and I'll bet you have to enter your room number before joining their network. Using an unsecured Wi-Fi location and hiding your IP address is the smarter way to go. It's a little like being in stealth mode."

"It's a good thing one of us is a criminal mastermind." Finn wiggled his eyebrows and I found his expression cuter than it should have been.

20

What is it about engaging in illegal activity that's just a little bit sexy? Okay, it probably isn't always sexy, but Finn had this whole bad-boy image going and I liked it. Mary Jane's email was pretty much typical day-to-day junk. Bill notifications, discount coupons, and flash-sale offers clogged her trash. However, the fact that she only had three unread messages in her inbox, among a slew of emails, told us that she regularly checked her account. To my disappointment, nothing looked all that promising. My foray into computer hacking looked like it was going to be a total bust. Talk about an anti-climactic experience. That is, until Finn checked MJ's drafts. It looked as if MJ had started a response to Sterling, but never sent it.

"Look at this," Finn said, turning the computer so I could read. We put our heads together.

My dearest MJ, I know you're a fan of poetry and love songs and I hope you find those in your life again. You have always held my heart, and I yours, but that is no longer the case. For that I am sorry, but it is the truth. You deserve someone to make you smile, to make you laugh, to make you feel the way that I feel right now. I love you enough to wish you that happiness.

THAT WAS IT. MJ's response remained blank. "What do you think this all means? Was he just breaking up with her or was this his way of saying goodbye?" Nothing in the letter directly said he was about to off himself, just that he felt his relationship with MJ was over.

"I'm really not sure."

We'd hoped a letter from Sterling would provide clarity, but we were mistaken.

~

FINN and I slept in the next morning after finishing the rest of the champagne and staying up late, video conferencing our friends and family to tell them the news. Aria's reaction was priceless and I couldn't wait to catch up with my girl.

I was in the middle of my usual morning routine of checking email and social media accounts when a news story caught my attention. I bolted upright in bed.

"Finn. Finn, wake up." I jostled him awake.

"What, what is it?"

"MJ. She's been arrested. Look!" I thrusted my phone in his face. A picture of Mary Jane being led into the courthouse in handcuffs dominated the screen. That got Finn's attention.

"What does it say?" I asked him.

"That she's confessed to attempting to murder Dr. Stewart."

"No way, let me see." I moved closer to the screen. Finn was right. "I can't believe she confessed."

"The article speculates that she dusted a handful of dishes and surfaces in his office with peanut flour."

"Talk about exacting revenge. Does the article say what happens next or how Brad is doing?"

"It doesn't, but I'm thinking she might be able to bond out. A judge might be sympathetic to her situation."

I shook my head, feeling sorry for MJ's family. They had already been through so much. As for MJ, I wasn't sure how I felt about her.

"That definitely puts a damper on the entire suicide angle."

"How so?" Finn handed me back my phone.

"Well, two things. I don't see MJ trying to kill Brad if there was any chance she knew Sterling killed himself, and I don't see Sterling killing himself and not leaving her a note." I thought back to the conversation I had overheard between Sterling and Mr. Aldrich. "I also don't see how Sterling saying he'd take care of it meant killing himself. More like he'd deal with the person responsible for killing Marissa."

"Okay, I can buy all that. So where does that leave us?"

I blew out a breath. "I have no idea." I felt completely defeated.

"Maybe if I take a shower, I'll be able to clear my head and figure it out."

It didn't work.

By late afternoon, I had moved on from simply jotting notes down on my phone's app to using full-fledged, color-coded notecards of all the key players and their motives.

Finn came back from a run and saw that I was still at it, rearranging the notecards to determine which story made the most sense. Honestly, it could have gone so many ways, and I was more confused than ever.

"Babe, why don't you take a break? Maybe a rest will help you figure it all out."

I had thought the same thing, but I just couldn't stand the thought of giving up when I felt so close to cracking the case. Finn sensed my hesitation.

"How about you agree to take a break and I'll book you a treatment at the spa downstairs? Maybe a manicure to show off that sparkly little rock you've got on your finger."

That was an idea I could get on board with. "Manicure *and* pedicure?"

"I'd say all that and more. With how stressful your week has been, I'll book you the works."

That did sound heavenly. I took one last look at the notecards scattered around the floor and agreed to the deal. I now knew by experience it was much nicer to receive a massage than to pretend to be the massage therapist giving one.

~

Tess was just finishing up with her nails when I walked around and sat down to have mine started.

"Hi, Tess. How are you?"

It took her a minute to place me. "It's Ziva, right?"

"That it is."

Tess spotted the sparkler on my finger and her eyes lit up. She made a whistling sound. "That's beautiful, darling. Is it new?" She grabbed my hand to inspect my ring.

"Just got it yesterday."

"Congratulations. My third husband gave me a ring just like that."

"Thanks so much. Have things settled down at work yet?"

"I don't know. I haven't been there much this week..." Tess trailed off, lost in her thoughts, and I didn't bother to pick up the conversation.

"Watch your ring around that one," my nail tech said to me once Tess left.

"What, why?"

"Notice none of us are wearing any jewelry around her." The three girls on the other side of the stations all raised their hands to show their naked wrists and fingers.

"Management won't let us toss her out, but we know she's stolen her fair share of jewelry from us and our clients. Only problem is we don't have any proof."

"No video surveillance or anything?" I looked around, trying to spot a security system.

"Not in the spa area, and she's never seen wearing the pieces throughout the hotel."

I never would've pegged Tess as a jewelry thief. Then I thought back to the graceful way that she moved and compared it to the person I saw sneaking around Marissa's dressing room on Saturday morning. My mouth dropped open. Sweet sugar, they could very well be one and the same.

Does that mean she also murdered Marissa and Sterling? I needed to find a way to set her up.

"I never would've said anything if you girls hadn't brought it up, but last week when I was at work with her, my necklace came up missing." I pulled my gold cross out from underneath my tank top. "As luck would have it, my fiancé and I came across it at a pawn shop on the other side of town."

"Girl, that's crazy," said the one nail tech.

"I know, totally random, and it gets better. I know for a fact that someone has been stealing jewelry from the DSC offices, and it could very well be her."

They all looked at one another in disbelief. "Shut up, girl. That is too coincidental. Let me get my manager," said the same tech.

"That's an excellent idea," I replied.

"Stacy, you have to hear this," one of the other girls told the manager when she joined us. I filled her in quickly and then said, "But I have an idea. You see that product line right there, Sugar and Sass?" I motioned to the wall display behind me. "That's me. I own that company. So, here's what I propose. We set up a VIP meet-and-greet for tomorrow night, maybe even a spa demo of my new product line. Heck, I could even debut my first signature fragrance. Tess has already seen my ring, and if she's as much of a klepto as we think she is, she won't be able to resist a chance to take a swipe at it. Only, we'll be ready with hidden cameras and security on standby. What do you all think?"

"I think it's a fabulous idea," said Stacy. "We can't afford to have her continuing to steal from our clients. The spa's going to get a bad reputation, and I can't let that happen."

"Great, let me just call my store manager and see what promo pieces we can whip up, and if you want to personally call your favorite clients and invite them, that would be great. I'm assuming you have Tess's phone number?"

"We do. Leave the guest list to us, and I'll make sure to have enough product available for purchasing."

"If it's okay with you, you could also offer the same special that DSC ran on my promo spot. It's just an idea."

"That's brilliant, and we can even tie-in that you were just on the show," Stacy added.

"Ah, you might want to skip that part. In case you haven't heard, it was a total disaster."

"Okay, we'll skip that, but we'll still advertise the deal and the debut of your new fragrance."

"Awesome, thanks!" Now I just needed to finish designing the fragrance and find a way to package it in the next twenty-four hours. Oh, and find out how I was going to get Tess to confess. Minor detail.

I told Finn my master plan when I was back in the hotel room. He just shook his head. "I know I should be surprised, seeing you were supposed to be down there relaxing, but I'm really not. What can I do to help?"

"I need to make a run back to the wellness store for some essential oils. My formula is just not right and I think I need lighter base notes. Can you see if you can find a replica of my ring? I'm all for setting Tess up, but I don't want to put my engagement ring in the line of fire in case she makes off with it and we don't catch her. It doesn't have to be exact. I don't think she got a good look at it. As long as the stone is pink and the band is gold, we should be good to go."

"On it."

"Thanks, babe." My notecards were calling to me, and this time I knew exactly how I was going to lay them out. The best way to take someone down was to know their weakness, and now we knew Tess's.

21

I had several bottles of essential oils lined up on the hotel room's desk, and a bit of a headache, when I finally gave in and called Izzy.

"Go with the jasmine." I stared at the open bottle of jasmine in front of me.

"Try mixing it with lime or sweet orange to cut down on the floral aspect, and hopefully it won't make you sneeze."

I tentatively mixed the two together with my sweet almond oil and took a whiff. It was perfect. "How do you do that?"

"It's a gift. Now, what else do you need?"

I closed my eyes for a moment. *Press release.* "Did we send something over for the spa to use for their guests?" I wanted to give them a bit of a script when calling to invite people for tonight.

"Done. I did it right after hanging up the phone with you yesterday."

"You know you're awesome, right?"

"Yes, I know I'm awesome. Now you just need to wrap this stuff up and get home so we can celebrate!"

"About that, there's something big I want to talk to you about when I get back."

"You mean about you giving me my own store?" After the jasmine trick, I shouldn't have been surprised. "Of course, I don't know the details of when this is all supposed to take place, but I'm pretty sure that's what my guides are trying to tell me."

"Your guides would be spot on. Finn did take that job down here, and we're thinking of opening another Sugar and Sass store down in Tampa. I'll probably bounce back and forth between the two for a while, but is that something you're even interested in?"

"Sweetie, I would love to manage my own store full time."

I found myself smiling like a fool because that was one piece of the puzzle that had to be locked down for the next phase to even be a possibility.

"Is that the right answer?"

"You know it. Now, about these murders, what can you tell me?" Since she was on a roll and I hadn't asked her yet, I thought it wouldn't hurt to give it a try.

"Oh no, don't ask me that. I don't deal with death and trying to hack into the spiritual guides of murderers. Gives me the creepy crawlies just thinking about it."

Well, it gave *me* the creepy crawlies when she put it that way.

"I can tell you though, just by reading you, that you're going to solve this and come out smelling like roses, or maybe it's jasmine I'm smelling."

"Ha ha, aren't you funny. I'll catch up with you in a little bit and let you know how tonight goes."

"I know you will. Take care, love."

My phone buzzed in my purse and I went to retrieve it while Finn drove around looking for a good place to eat. We had a couple of hours to kill before tonight's big event and Finn thought to fill it with food. Honestly, I had been craving Thai since Brad brought it up. It was like peanut sauce had become the forbidden fruit, and I couldn't wait to indulge.

I looked at my phone and saw that it was Cee Cee calling. I answered it immediately.

"Hey, Cee Cee, what's up?"

"I found out something interesting."

"Interesting, like how?"

"First, tell me how it went with Dr. Stewart. We never got a chance to catch up. Then I'll tell you what I know. I have a new theory and I'm hoping your impression of Dr. Stewart will corroborate it."

I told Cee Cee straight up what I thought of Brad, skipping the part about MJ barging into my appointment. It was sort of a moot point now. "So, yeah, it's not him. I'd even go as far as to say that he's being framed."

"Okay, so that's what I was also thinking. Working that angle, I stopped investigating Brad and instead focused on Marissa's and Sterling's coworkers. I think I might have found our red herring. Tess filed bankruptcy."

"Bankruptcy? But she lives such a lavish lifestyle."

"Not for long. She's broke. That hotel she's living in? It's because she lost her condo. I saw the tax liens for myself at the county court house."

"So, she's living at the hotel on credit?"

"Maybe, but she won't be for long. I'm betting her credit's in the toilet and her reputation is about to follow."

"Her motive just shot up like a rocket." As if it wasn't already, with the suspected thefts.

"Right?"

"It's not just that she was mad that her contract wasn't renewed, she was desperate."

"Desperate and with nothing to lose," Cee Cee replied.

"Maybe she thought that if she killed Sterling and Marissa, the network would keep her. They would have to, after all, right?" I thought Cee Cee would know more about this than I would.

"Probably. Viewers don't like it when you shake things up too much. They'd probably want to keep Tess to maintain some sense of normalcy."

"And she could keep her reign as the Queen of the Daytime Shopping Channel." From the sound of it, that's pretty much all she has left—a title. "Have you shared this information with anyone?" I asked.

"Just my new producer, Skip."

"Skip the Producer?"

"Yeah, you know him?

He's..." I thought of how to describe the man, "a bit quirky, isn't he? He seems more like a mad scientist to me than a television producer. I could totally see him mixing vials of green goo in a chemistry lab."

"Yeah, I can see where you get that from. I just started working with him. He jumped the DSC ship this last week and our network picked him up immediately." I had a feeling a lot of people would be jumping ship, especially until these murders were solved.

FINN GOT the gist of it by listening to my conversation with Cee Cee. We scarfed down heaping bowls of spicy noodles while discussing how Tess tied it all together.

"I'm over the whole Dr. Stewart angle." I had a moment of pang for the good doctor as he couldn't indulge in this peanut-sauce goodness.

"I agree with you that the whole thing looks like a setup."

"Right, and it's something Tess could easily have pulled off. She was at the gala. I saw her there with my own eyes. She also had the anger issues, and the most to gain. She is also the most desperate. I can see her being the one to go back to the scene Saturday morning and steal that necklace."

"She had the motive and nothing to lose."

"Right, Marissa and Claire had already caused her to slip from her throne and she was on her way out. Come to think of it, both Sterling and Marissa screwed her over. Sterling for not fighting for her contract renewal, and Marissa, a girl she considered her protégé, for stealing her air time. It would seem fitting for Tess to stab Marissa in the back and do Sterling in as a bonus."

"All because of a job?"

"DSC was more than a job to her. It was her life. You should've heard her talk about it, she truly felt she had given them everything and they repaid her by giving her the boot when younger girls came on board and boosted the ratings."

"What else do you know about her?"

"Besides the fact that she appeared to have a love affair with gin, and she wasn't too sad to hear about either host's murder?"

"And you took her off the suspect list why?"

Why *had* I taken her off the list? I couldn't come up with a solid answer. "It doesn't matter. We have her now." I was ready to take her down.

22

I walked the floor of the spa, greeting guests and looking more confident than I felt. I managed to drag Finn out shopping before tonight's event for a new outfit. My soft-pink chiffon sleeveless blouse with the ruffles down the middle set off the fake ring on my finger nicely. I completed the look with a pair of white capri pants and my favorite cork heels. My hair was pulled back into a high ponytail and I chose not to wear my cross necklace to avoid giving Tess a chance to question how I got it back, or to take another swipe at it.

Everything looked perfect. Even my graphic designer had been able to come through in a pinch and create the perfect script font for my new signature scent, Dreamfields. I had been able to print out the name onto clear labels, which I then smoothed onto little glass roller bottles of the fragrance.

Stacy was ecstatic with how well the turnout had been. I understood her enthusiasm, but it would've totally been a bust if Tess hadn't shown up. Halfway through the events, as I eyed the hors d'oeuvres making their way around again,

Tess made an entrance. She wore a royal purple belt dress that made her look not a day over fifty, and her skin was more radiant than normal. If she didn't have such sticky fingers and homicidal tendencies, I would've considered hiring her as a spokesperson.

"*Show time*," I said to myself under my breath. Stacy caught my eye at about the same time and watched as I walked over to make small talk with Tess. I thought it would be best to get the ring in front of her again and give her plenty of opportunity to make her move. I could only hope that the cameras we had hidden in strategic locations would catch the moment of theft.

"Tess, so good of you to stop in. I heard you were a top client here."

"I wouldn't miss it for the world," she replied and it may have been my imagination, but I swear she looked down to case out my ring. Finn was monitoring a live feed and promised to text me in case I missed anything. I felt relieved to have him guarding my back, but I was still nervous. I would have loved to have the police on standby, but we all knew that Detective Blackwell was not a friend of mine. Hotel security had been alerted that Tess would be present. Truthfully, that was all Stacy had had to tell them. It seemed like everyone was well aware of her reputation. The one thing I hadn't yet been able to figure out was why Tess killed Sterling. I figured she had eliminated Marissa to secure her top spot in the network. Of course, she wouldn't have had to if she'd known that Marissa was already passed up for the promotion. But something told me it wasn't common knowledge. Marissa wouldn't have gone around the studio announcing it to everyone, and I couldn't see Mr. Aldrich making it public information either. The best I could figure was she killed Marissa in an all-out cat fight and Sterling figured it out, which is why he said he would take care of it, only it was Tess who took care of him. As for the diamond I saw Tess steal from Marissa's dressing room, she must've snatched it from Marissa's dead body and hid it after the police arrived and she realized she wouldn't be able to leave the studio with the necklace in her possession, for fear of being searched. I must've seen her on Saturday morning when she came back to retrieve it. I had put two and two together and realized the necklace that Marissa had worn was the same one she had on in the beach photo on Dr. Stewart's desk.

As I watched Tess work the room, I realized she'd found a way to touch almost everyone present, whether by a hand on the shoulder, a quick hug, or a rub on the back. It felt to me like she was taking inventory to see what possessions people had on, trying to decide how she would go about lifting them. I also noticed that all the spa staff had sported their best jewelry for the occasion, just as a little extra temptation. I really hoped they wore fakes as well.

I must confess: The biggest struggle so far that night was keeping myself from hitting up the dessert table. The hotel's patisserie had done a fabulous job supplying the desserts. Their display made Mrs. Morrison's kitchen look amateur. I'd already told myself that if this all went down how I hoped it would, I was rewarding myself with one of those heavenly looking buttercream-frosted cookies. Finn texted me a moment later: "*Eyes on the prize, babe.*" Yeah, it was that easy to see where my thoughts were.

If it wasn't for the fact that I was trying to catch a murderous thief, I would've had a very enjoyable evening. That is, until the power went out. My self-control, where the desserts were concerned, was just about broken. I noticed Tess looking content talking with the head of security, who happened to stop in for an update. I figured it was a safe time to sneak over and steal a sugar cookie. My hand was on the delicious dessert when the entire spa was plunged into darkness. A couple of women shrieked, a few even giggled, but I knew it was no laughing matter. I felt a hand on mine, slipping the ring off my finger, despite my hyper-vigilant state. Then I heard the person take off running. I wasn't going to let Tess get away that easily.

I kicked off my heels and gave chase. Only problem was, being in the pitch black meant that I ran right into the dessert table. Tarts and sugar cookies flew in the air, at least I think they did. I know I stepped in something cold and squishy with my bare toes that felt an awful lot like custard. I might have also elbowed someone in the gut if the "*oomph*" sound I heard was any indication.

I couldn't stop to apologize. Tess was making her way to the back of the store and out the back exit, I was sure of it. In the storage room, she tipped boxes over as she ran, no doubt trying to trip me up. Even in the darkness, I hurdled those obstacles like a track star. Tess's heels click-clacked on the tile floor and I caught up to her right about the same time I remembered that Tess hadn't worn high heels. I grabbed the woman by the arm just as she busted out the back door. I came face-to-face with Claire.

"Girl, you have some explaining to do," I said, not letting go of her arm. It was the same quote my mother used to say to me when I got busted doing something wrong. I hoped it scared Claire as much as it had me in my youth. Finn caught up with us a second later, with Stacy right behind him. Claire saw the look on all of our faces and knew she was busted.

"Before you even think about lying, know that we caught you on camera hitting the breaker box," Finn said.

"I'm sorry. I don't know what I was thinking. Sometimes social situations make me anxious and I just panic."

"Say what?" said Stacy. "You couldn't just go out the front door?"

"Yeah, and I bet if we call the cops and search you, we'll find my ring in your possession."

Claire stumbled out a handful of words and none of them made much sense.

"Can you give us a minute?" I said to Finn and Stacy. They both stepped away.

"Listen, you have to talk to me because as it stands right now, I'm about to call the police and have them charge you with murder. Stealing my ring is the least of your worries." My rationale still stood, only it was Claire over Tess.

"I swear, I didn't kill anyone."

"And you didn't steal anything, either, right? If that's the case, I'm sure you wouldn't mind if I asked your coworkers if they're missing any jewelry. Oh, and not to mention the fact that I saw you steal the diamond out of Marissa's dressing room Saturday morning. Imagine how that would look for you to be found with that brilliant bauble." Claire's face turned ashen. It was obvious she hadn't thought of that. And then the woman started crying. It was as if she knew how much I hated when people cried.

I was about to apologize and put the whole thing behind me, and I probably would've if she hadn't started talking. "I'm sorry, I never meant for it to get like this. It's just, maintaining this lifestyle, trying to make it in this business, is not cheap."

"So, you became a thief?"

"Well, my parents were never going to help me out. TV's not a wholesome career. It wasn't until recently that I've been able to even make rent, let alone afford the shoes, the hair, the clothes. What else could I do?"

"Get a second job? Do something more, I don't know, respectable?"

"Please, Ziva, I'm begging you. If they find out, my career will be over. I swear that I never killed anyone."

I knew Claire was right, her career would be over, but I wasn't sure what the right thing to do was. "How'd you get Marissa's necklace?"

"I lifted it from her during cocktail hour. I'm sorry. I know it was wrong." Claire looked around as if waiting for the police to swoop in any second. "I'll give it all back. I promise. Your ring, Marissa's necklace, Sterling's watch, everything."

"You stole Sterling's watch, too?"

"It was supposed to be a party trick, at the gala, but then I saw that it was a Rolex."

"What in the world is wrong with you?"

"I'm so, so sorry. I swear, I'll join Thieves Anonymous or take a class, anything, just don't call the police. Here, come with me."

I shrugged my shoulders back at Finn. Stacy had already disappeared back inside to regain order. I followed Claire back to her car. Inside, she pulled a small lockbox from under the driver's seat. A cable, wrapped through the loop of the box and around the metal track of her seat, kept it in place. She rolled out the combination with her thumb and twisted the lock open. Now here was a pirate's booty. I didn't need it all, heck I didn't even know who it all belonged to, but I took back Marissa's necklace and Sterling's watch. I turned the watch over in my hand and read the inscription: *Every second, every day — MJ*. I knew I needed to give the watch back to Sterling's wife. If I called the police, who knew how long it would take for them to return the property. I thought MJ deserved it sooner than that. She needed a chance at closure.

"Go, get out of here. And I swear, if I ever hear about you doing anything like this again, I will call the police in a heartbeat."

"I swear, I won't. Promise. Oh, and your ring." Claire went to retrieve it from her pocket.

"Keep it. It's a fake. Maybe it'll help you remember to keep your promise."

Claire sobbed and thanked me profusely before hopping into her car and jetting off.

"Do you think that was the right thing to do?" Finn asked when I walked over to him. I shrugged my shoulders. I wasn't sure. "What are you going to do with those?" he asked.

"The watch? For sure, give it back to Sterling's wife. The same goes for the necklace. I know Dr. Stewart would want it back."

"Yeah, and you can't be found with it, either." Of course, I hadn't thought of that, but Finn was so right on that point.

23

"Now what?" Finn asked.

He seemed to be feeling just as melancholy as I was. We solved the case of the jewelry thief but still hadn't caught the killer. We were sitting outdoors, poolside, with a couple of drinks—chai latte for me and a black coffee for him. The sun had set and the pool area was pretty quiet. The only light was the glow of the underwater pool lights and the little white lights that sparkled in the surrounding trees.

"I don't know. Do we just go home?"

"And leave the case unsolved?"

I shrugged my shoulders. We really had nothing keeping us here anymore, but we had a life to live back home.

"You'd be okay with that?"

"Ugh, probably not, but it sounds like a promising idea, doesn't it?"

Finn took a drink of his coffee and I did the same.

Then I had an idea. "You know, who says it still isn't Tess? Just because she didn't steal Marissa's necklace doesn't mean she didn't kill her."

Finn looked at me like I was a genius. We were both up and on our feet. "Where do you want to go?" he asked.

"The bar. It seems to be a favorite locale for her."

Apparently, the pool had been quiet because everyone was in the bar.

"Oh, sweet sugar, it wasn't this busy last time I was here." Big difference between Sunday night and Thursday night. It was clear Tess wasn't sitting at the bar, but that didn't mean she wasn't nearby.

"You check out the private booths against the wall, and I'll walk up the middle and hit the ladies' room."

"Sounds good." Finn headed in one direction and I in the other.

When we met in the middle, neither one of us had spotted her. I looked over at the bar once more. I motioned to Mitch, the same bartender from earlier in the week who had agreed to take Tess up to her room. "He knows her."

I walked over to the bar and waited to catch his eye. "Hey, it's Mitch, right?"

"Yeah, what can I do for you?" Mitch held up his finger to the other bartender to let him know he'd be right there.

"Really quick, I was just wondering if you saw Tess tonight."

"Yeah, actually I did."

"You did? Awesome. Is she here?"

"No, she stopped in about an hour ago to say goodbye."

"Say what?"

"She said she was leaving town for a while and wasn't sure when she'd be back."

"Did she say where she was going?"

"Nope, and I had to let her go after that. Be there in a minute!" Mitch hollered over his shoulder.

"Okay, well, thanks," I said. Mitch slapped his hand on the bar as a goodbye and walked away.

I rounded on Finn. "Okay, let's roll."

"Where are we going?"

"I don't know, race off to the airport and see if we can track Tess down?"

"You know for a fact that she's planning to take off by plane?"

"No, but—"

"Do you have a plan for getting back in the boarding area?" Sure, I had a plan, and Finn read me like a book. "Ziva, it's not worth buying a plane ticket when we have no plans to go anywhere, just for a five-minute conversation with Tess."

I knew Finn had a point, but I couldn't simply drop the trail yet.

"I have an idea: How about I call the police and leave an anonymous tip. I'll tell them that I have compelling evidence that Tess killed Marissa and Sterling, and she's about to board a plane and take it with her. Let the police do their thing. I'm sure they'll have a way to stop her, or someone can meet her when she lands. We've done our part."

I nodded but wasn't so confident.

"Come on, let's go back upstairs to our room."

I gave Finn the look that said, I'm *so* not in the mood. "Nothing like that. I bought you a couple wedding magazines when I ran out this morning. Figured it would help you get your mind off things and we can start getting some ideas."

"I'm not sure if I should be impressed or worried. You're not going to turn into a groomzilla on me, are you?"

"I will try not to. No promises."

BACK IN THE ROOM, I couldn't settle down, even with the bridal magazines. Something was still bothering me about the case. It wasn't just Tess. The answers were right in front of my face, but a big mental block was preventing me from seeing them.

"You mind if I go for a walk?"

"No, go ahead, babe. Take your phone, though, and be careful. It's late."

"Will do, love you." I walked out of the hotel and into the warm night air. I was glad I had grabbed a sweater. Even though it was still seventy degrees, the ocean breeze was a bit chilly. I knew where I needed to go to get the answers, even if I didn't want to. The secret lied at the beach where Sterling's body was found, I was sure of it. I crossed my fingers in hopes I wouldn't find any other dead bodies.

As I walked along the sand, I wondered if there was any way I could prove Tess was the murderer. Right now, all I had was a theory. I kicked off my sandals and held the straps in my hand as I made my way across the sand. *Why the beach, Sterling? Why did you come here?* I found myself walking down the pier, scanning the area for answers, but all I saw were a couple of other people taking late-night strolls.

From the top of the pier, I looked over to where Sterling's body had been found by the lifeguard tower. In the distance, I could barely make her out, but I was almost certain it was the person I had inherently been looking for. She was standing in the lifeguard tower, overlooking the ocean. I thought she might be crying, but it was impossible to tell from this far away in the darkness. I quickly walked back down to the end of the pier, keeping her in my sight, hoping she wouldn't leave before I had a chance to speak with her.

I jogged across the sand, wind whipping in my hair as a storm blew in offshore. The woman never heard me approach until I was too close. MJ turned to look at me and, for the first time, I saw true fear in her eyes. I hadn't expected that. Instinctively, I whipped my head around in search for the danger and saw the revolver in her hand. *Sweet sugar, what did I just walk into?*

"This is where we were married. Did you know that?"

I tried to follow MJ's conversation. "Uh, yeah, I mean, I knew you were married at the beach," I said, recalling the photo Finn and I saw at her house.

"I had him meet me here where I begged and pleaded with him, forgave him, and he still dismissed me. Just like her. Oh, what did I do?" MJ's last words came out as a loud wail.

"Honey, it'll be okay." Truthfully, it probably wouldn't be, but I was thinking that reassurance was the smart way to go, given the circumstances. My eyes darted between MJ's face and the gun that shook in her hand. She looked up at me and the fear that had been in her eyes quickly changed to anger.

"I hated her. She thought she was so perfect, that the world owed her everything and she could take whatever she wanted. I begged her to leave my husband alone, to leave our family alone, and she laughed at me. Laughed at me! And then she walked away. That was it, like she couldn't be bothered by me. I just grabbed that shovel and dug it as hard as I could into her back. I can't even remember if she screamed. But she deserved it."

I wasn't sure what I expected MJ to say, but it wasn't that, and she wasn't done.

"I ran before I could think of what to do and then I saw you and knew I couldn't leave, so I waited. I waited for you to find her, and then when you ran out, I ran over and yanked the shovel out of her back." The look in MJ's eyes had shifted once more, this time to a cold-blooded killer. My cell phone buzzed in my pocket, reminding me that I had it on me. Of course, now wasn't the time to take a call, not with crazy lady here confessing to a murder, quite possibly two.

I took the phone out of my pocket anyway and looked at the screen quickly to dismiss it. "And Sterling?" I asked while quickly reading the screen. Cee Cee had sent me two words: "*Botulinum poisoning.*"

"You killed him with Botox?" I said it more as a question than a statement. MJ looked surprised that I knew. I held up my phone. "It's the latest breaking news." I wasn't sure if taunting a murderer was the right thing to do, but I didn't want her to get any ideas that she could kill me and be rid of the problem. "It's only a matter of time before they trace it back to you." I remembered seeing the vials of Botox and needles in her bathroom drawer.

I swear, right at that moment, the woman totally flipped her lid and lunged at me. I grabbed her wrist and squeezed hard, flinging the gun down to the sand below. I'm not sure which one of us was screaming more, but it was a cat fight on steroids. The woman's strength was intense. But I had a secret weapon, and it was in the shape of a palm-sized pink stone. I reached into my back pocket and took out the quartz Izzy had given me earlier in the week. With one swift move, I smacked MJ on the back of her head with it. It was just enough to stun her and enabled me to roll over and sit on her chest. She gave an "*oomph*" as the air left her lungs. By this time, a small crowd had gathered and people were shouting for us to separate. I managed to wheeze out, "Murderer, Sterling, Marissa," between breaths. Someone must have believed me because the cops showed up not more than two minutes later. For all I knew, they had already been on their way. I never did find out, but I was grateful they came, even if it meant dealing with Detective Blackwell again.

~

Detective Blackwell didn't look pleased to see me, but she lightened up when I explained it all to her. She still didn't like me, but at least she no longer thought I was a murderer. Finn met me at the beach, and I knew we'd be heading back to the police station shortly.

"What I still don't understand is why she tried to kill Brad. She knew he wasn't the killer," I said to Finn.

"It was her best defense. No one would think she was a killer if she appeared to be distraught enough to try and kill the case's prime suspect."

"I guess that's true."

"A charge of attempted murder looks pretty good compared to being charged with double homicide."

"And Tess is completely innocent." I felt like I had to send her some sort of handwritten apology, even though she never knew what we suspected of her. "I was completely wrong there. Of course, that's not the first time."

"No, but you figured it out in the end, like always, my little Sherlock."

"Does that make you Watson?"

"If that means being your partner in crime, then you can call me whatever you want."

I would have to remember that. "What do you say we

finish this police business and then go properly celebrate our engagement?"

"Babe, you know all you ever have to do is ask." Finn did his sexy trademark eyebrow raise and I shook my head, as I imagined I'd be doing every day for the rest of my life.

PEDICURES & PREJUDICE

BEAUTY SECRETS BOOK 4

Available October 17th, 2017

PREORDER NOW

myBook.to/pedicures

ABOUT THE AUTHOR

Stephanie Damore is a mystery author with a soft spot for romance and humor, too. She loves all things girlie with a dollop of danger and has a strong affinity for the color pink (especially in diamonds and champagne.) Her books feature fearless females, a little bit of love, a few laughs, and a whole lot of whodunit. She hopes her stories keep you guessing and laughing all the way until the end.

I love to hear from my readers!

www.stephaniedamore.com
steph.damore@gmail.com

25025320R00110

Printed in Poland
by Amazon Fulfillment
Poland Sp. z o.o., Wrocław